ARAZHI

TAMSIN LEY

Paperback version
ISBN-13: 9781950027415
Copyright © 2021 Twin Leaf Press

Georgie flinched as the black lab on her grooming table shook water from his fur. The big oaf was one of the lucky ones headed to the feed store for adoption day, and she'd volunteered to help groom and transport them from the shelter. She wiped her glasses off on her sleeve and finished rinsing the pup, who thanked her with one of his signature slobbery kisses. If she wasn't living in a tiny one-bedroom apartment with her dad at the moment, she would've considered adopting him herself, but there was barely room for the two of them as it was.

In the nearby kennels, a dog started barking, which soon escalated into a chorus. The Jack Russell Terrier Lora was grooming on the next table over started crying, writhing against the leash. The poor baby had anxiety issues, and Lora tried to distract it with a squeaky toy.

"I think you're stressing her even more, Lora," said Georgie, making a face at the added noise.

At the third dog washing station, Maise had already finished with an older German Shepherd who now lay placidly at her feet. She owned Yappy Hour, the pet boarding and grooming business they were using to clean up the dogs, and was a pro with the wash station. She leaned against the table, long dark ringlets obscuring her face as she looked at her phone. "What about this one, Georgie? Intergalactic Dating Agency seeks capable human to coordinate first ever alien matchmaking event. All applications considered."

"You've got to be kidding," said Lora, ceasing her squeaky toy distraction and looking at Georgie. "Aliens?"

Extraterrestrials hadn't been seen on Earth since a singular appearance over forty years ago—if that was even to be believed. The ships had landed at Beijing Daxing International Airport in China, spoken to government officials there, and departed again before the other nations could even respond. Despite photographs and eyewitness accounts, many people believed the visit had been a hoax—a myth created by governments to justify spending on defense and outlandish space research.

Yet in the years since, people still claimed to have been abducted, including Georgie's mom. Her mom had died several years ago from a head injury after falling from a ladder, but Georgie'd always wanted to believe her mother's story.

"Maybe they're checking in on us," Georgie said.

"To ask for dates to the movies? How desperate can they be?" Lora snorted. "Keep scrolling, Maise."

"No, wait. I want to know more," said Georgie, wiping her hands off on a towel.

If this was an actual, paying gig, she couldn't dismiss it without at least reading the fine print. She'd been trying to get her event planning business off the ground for months now, but every time she thought she had a lead, someone snagged the contract out from under her. The only people who said yes couldn't pay her, and one guy who wanted a bar mitzvah for his son had even had the balls to say she should be grateful for the "exposure" planning his son's event would get her. Asshole.

Problem was, she was desperate enough to consider it. Since her divorce, she'd been living with her dad to save money, sinking all her savings into getting her business off the ground while working part time as a cashier at the grocery store. She had to do something soon, or she was going to go crazy.

"Maybe it's just a cosplay party or something. Let me see your phone." She held out her hand.

Maise handed over her cell, and Georgie looked over the advertisement. An alien matchmaking event did sound hokey, but it wouldn't hurt to ask for more information and submit a proposal. Heck, an alien-themed party could be really fun. She typed in her email address and handed the phone back.

"How cool would it be to plan the first ever party with actual aliens?" asked Maise, pocketing the phone and grabbing a towel to help Georgie with the lab.

"I just want to know how much they'll pay." Georgie fixed a collar around the dog's neck and led him to the floor.

"You couldn't pay me enough to go on a date with an alien." Lora scooped the shivering terrier into her arms.

As they headed to the shelter's van to load the dogs for transport, the breeze coming off the pulp factory made Georgette want to gag. It was particularly bad today. She'd just closed the lab into a kennel and shut the door when her phone pinged with an incoming email. She glanced at it.

"It's them," she said, surprised to have a response so quickly, then read the email out loud. "Thank you for your interest in the Intergalactic Dating Agency. Please send proposed Earth time frame, location and cultural requirements."

Lora readjusted her sagging auburn ponytail. "Earth time frame? Really? They're certainly playing up the alien angle, aren't they?"

"Just staying in character, I guess." Georgie chuckled. A plan was already forming in her head. "At least I know they want me to keep things weird."

"What the heck are cultural requirements?" asked Maise.

"I don't know, but it sounds fun." Georgie squinted at the fine print at the bottom of the email. It was hard to read, so she expanded the text.

Her jaw dropped. "Holy crap, listen to this! Upon acceptance, the coordinator will be paid ten thousand Earth credits in the monetary unit of their choosing plus expenses upon receipt."

"Earth credits?" asked Maise as she climbed into the van's front seat. "What are those?"

"I think they mean I can choose dollars or yen or whatever currency I want." Georgie bit her lip. "And look, the return email is from a dot gov site." She let out a slow breath. "I think this really is a solicitation from aliens."

Lora scrunched one eye doubtfully and moved to the driver's side. "Highly questionable."

Questionable or not, Georgie needed the money. "I have an idea. Let's host a charity auction where aliens—or alien wannabes or whatever—bid on dates, and the proceeds benefit the shelter. The client foots the bill for the party, with food, dancing, and booze. The aliens meet women, and the shelter earns some money. Win-win!"

"But who are you going to auction?" asked Maise, scooting across the bench and buckling into the middle seat.

Georgie gave her a devious smile and climbed in behind her. "People who support the animal shelter, of course."

Lora shook her head and started the engine. "Count me out. I'm not into green slime."

"They're not slimy," insisted Georgie. "They look sort of human. See?" She did a quick search and found one of the old images that had been all over the news. A slim alien with bluish skin looked into the camera with big eyes.

"They're sort of cute," said Maise.

Lora glanced at the image, then put the van into drive. "He looks like my grandpa."

Georgie released a heavy sigh. "I'm not asking you to marry one, Lora. Just go out to dinner. Or coffee. Look at it as an opportunity to make new friends."

"I usually do more than make friends on my dates." Lora gave her a sardonic look.

"Slut." Maise elbowed her in the ribs with a smile.

Lora laughed. "Whatever."

"Please?" begged Georgie. "I really need this contract."

"I'll run security for you. You might need someone to fend off death rays or something." Lora was a police officer and always assumed there'd be trouble.

"I can hire security," Georgie said. "I need women for the auction."

Lora raised an eyebrow. "Who says they want women?"

"Oh." Georgie opened up her email. "You're right. I'd better ask."

"What about you?" asked Maise. "Are you entering?"

"I have to run things." Georgie was already researching possible venues, caterers, permits…

Lora snorted and turned onto the highway. "Right. The perfect excuse."

Georgie looked up. "Fine. If I enter the auction, will you agree to do it, too?"

"Can I bring my dogs?" asked Maise. "If it's a pet event, we should include pets."

"Great idea," Georgie said. "We can hold it at Covey Park."

"Aliens, come run with our animals at the dog park!" Lora called toward the ceiling.

"So you'll help?" asked Georgie, batting her eyes beseechingly at her friend.

"I guess," said Lora. "But at the first sign of slime, I'm out."

Georgie finished drafting her proposal while they drove. Normally, she would take this home to think about it. But she'd had opportunity snatched out from under her too often.

This time, she was going to be first.

She hit send and set her phone on her lap. Once she had a contract, she'd worry about getting more volunteers for the auction.

To her surprise, her phone buzzed before they'd even reached the feed store. She swallowed, hardly able to believe the response. *Your terms are acceptable. Women matches only. Please find your fee in your monetary storage account. Additional funds available upon receipt. Send updates to this address.*

Wondering how they'd accessed her bank account, she logged on to find she was now ten thousand dollars richer. "Holy shit," she breathed. "I just got the contract."

"You did?" Maise asked.

Georgie showed her the bank balance.

"Wow! That was fast!" Maise grinned and raised her hand for a high five.

Georgie gleefully smacked her palm as reality settled in.

She had an event to plan.

2

*P*rince Arazhi descended the ramp from his private ship onto the dark stone tiles of the landing pad outside the palace. As he walked, his limbs shifted, becoming heavily muscled to match his mother's species, while his blue-skinned features coalesced into the bored-but-responsible look he tended to wear for his family. He'd received an urgent request to attend his father, Emperor Ozhin, and he wasn't happy he'd been dragged away from his latest dalliance with a Hypawa female with eyes like liquid magma and a mouth just as hot.

Like most of his liaisons, she'd hoped to secure a prince as a mate. And like all of his liaisons, he'd enjoyed the game, teaching her how to entice a partner without allowing himself to be enticed. An all-male species, Kirenai were well known across the galaxy as being able to bring great pleasure to their partners, using their empathic Iki'i senses to know exactly what a female desired. But Arazhi had no intention of attaching himself to a jealous, power-hungry female.

Guards stood posted outside the palace courtyard, their various bipedal shapes encased in full body armor, despite the heat. They greeted him with nods as he passed. He strode through the gate into the courtyard where towering blue happa fronds shaded the mossy path to the palace's main door.

A bondservant met him at the threshold. "Welcome home, my prince. Would you like me to prepare your room?"

"I won't be staying, but thank you." He intended to go straight back to the Hypawa's waiting arms once this meeting was over.

Arazhi strode down the arched stone hallway toward the throne room. Even when there was no court in session, his father preferred to conduct life from the vantage of his throne, and Arazhi was surprised to find the emperor's dais vacant.

A teal-skinned guard in traditional happa bark body armor stood at the base of the platform. He pointed toward the back to the royal chambers.

Unshielded anxiety pulsed from that direction, nudging his Iki'i senses, and Arazhi moved toward the door, concern building in his chest; most of the time he had to be nearby to sense someone's emotions.

The royal sitting room was vacant, and the doors to the bedroom stood open. The fruity scent of regeneration fluid filled the air. Concern transformed to worry, and he hurried forward.

"...can't be certain," someone in the bedchamber was saying, followed by a murmur he didn't catch.

Inside the chamber, Arazhi found Elthos, the royal healer and the emperor's most trusted advisor, standing near a regeneration pod that must've been brought in from the clinic, pink-scaled features as unreadable as ever. Arazhi's dam sat next to it, one alabaster hand resting on the lip of the gray, trough-like container that brimmed with green regeneration fluid.

Arazhi's heart constricted. Kirenai required periods of rest when they allowed their bodies to relax into their natural, amorphous state, but regen fluid was reserved for the seriously ill or injured who couldn't maintain a humanoid form to consume sustenance.

He hurried forward. "What's going on, Damma? Is Father hurt?"

His damma rose, a tight smile on her pale white face. She was a Vatosangan, small and slight, with deep blue hair and rounded features. "My child, we're so glad you're here."

The regen fluid in the pod roiled as his father's pale blue face appeared just above the surface. "Hello, my son." The emperor's usually melodious voice had a gravelly quality. "It's good you've come."

"Tell me what happened." Arazhi leaned over to look into the pod. The blue, amoeba-like form floating inside showed no outward signs of illness or damage.

Damma shrugged, blue lashes damp with unshed tears. "He cannot keep to his upright form. The healers say he's been poisoned."

"Poisoned?" Arazhi sucked in a breath. That explained the regen fluid. He looked to the nearby healer. "When? By who? Is there an antidote?"

"We are working on one," Elthos said with a bow. As a Qalqan, he possessed a machine-like calm that was immune to a Kirenai's Iki'i, but a Qalqan's objectivity also made them the best healers in the galaxy. "The palace guards are investigating suspects."

Damma nodded to the healer. "Thank you, Elthos. Please keep me updated on what you find."

"Of course, empress. I'll get back to work." Elthos bowed again and turned to leave.

Arazhi watched his father's face dip below the surface and back up again. Normally, his father was excellent at shielding his Iki'i, but pain now leaked from him in undulating waves.

Damma rose from her cushion and looped her arm through his, drawing his attention. "You must produce an heir immediately."

Arazhi bit his lip. This was not the discussion he'd prepared for, especially now that he knew his father was ill. "I don't want to talk about that now, Damma. I'm still young, and I've met no one who makes my shape want to settle, let alone solidify." That was only partly true—there had been a female on Sireta Prime who'd kept him enthralled for almost two irns when he was younger. But she'd continually compared him to other men, no matter how he adjusted his form, and eventually left to marry a G'nax nobleman. He'd avoided that sector of space ever since.

Emperor Ozhin sighed. "The Senburu are on the verge of a coup. They want to nominate a new successor to the throne."

The Senburu were powerful merchants who dominated the galactic consortium of planets and disagreed with the emperor's trade policies. They'd been trying to relegate his father's position to nothing but a figurehead since before Arazhi was born. "They can't do that. The planetary governors support our dynasty."

Damma took his hand. "Kirenai are bonding less frequently, and even bonded pairs produce fewer and fewer offspring. Everyone wants to be sure the royal line is secure. The consortium won't allow you to ascend the throne without an heir."

"That's ludicrous." He pulled his hand free. "I have plenty of time to produce an heir."

Most Kirenai waited until late in their long life to settle, enjoying their capacity to assume different forms as long as possible. Once a Kirenai bonded, his form would permanently assume the most pleasing shape for his mate.

Voice strained, his father said, "The consortium has already put forth Senbur Aguno as a candidate."

Arazhi stiffened. Aguno was his father's second cousin and only known blood relative. "He would turn on you like that?"

"He's found a mate," Damma said softly. "And it's rumored she's already with child."

Arazhi frowned. He'd seen Aguno at a recent ball, and there'd been no mention of a mate, let alone a child. "How is that possible?"

"His mate's from a planet called Earth, where the females are said to be like ijin'en, going into estrus and out again as easily as breathing," said his father.

Ijin'en were herd animals that symbolized stupidity. "What sort of heir can such a union produce?" Arazhi scoffed. "The Senburu can't possibly consider such a species worthy of the throne."

"Earth's inhabitants are primitive, but not unintelligent," his father said.

Damma added, "Their planet was supposed to be closed to trade, protected until the species was more technologically developed. But since it's now public knowledge that Aguno has successfully bred with one, your father was forced to authorize limited social access."

Arazhi scowled. "If the planet was supposed to be closed, how did Aguno end up with a mate? We should arrest him for breaking the trade edict and be done with it."

"It's not that easy." Damma's voice held a note of disgust. "Aguno rescued her from black market slave traders. Apparently, they've been abducting Earth females and forcing them into servitude without contracts."

Arazhi's throat tightened. Slavery was legal in this part of the galaxy, but only if a person enslaved themselves

—and they always had the right to buy back their own contracts. Most of the palace bondservants entered contracts merely to enjoy the prestige of working for the emperor, and would be retired with a stipend when they were no longer able to work.

"What's important now is how this affects our dynasty," his father grated out, voice becoming more gravelly every time he spoke. "Humans are capable of producing children without a permanent bond."

Arazhi shook his head. His father must be delusional. Kirenai could only reproduce after forming a permanent bond. "Didn't you say Aguno was mated?"

Damma answered, "He is, but other rescued females had already been impregnated without being mated to their captors."

"Are you certain the progeny are Kirenai?" Arazhi asked.

Kirenai could breed with a female of any species, producing male children that were always purely Kirenai, with empathic and shapeshifting abilities. The female progeny were of their mother's species, although a few did also inherit Kirenai Iki'i power.

"The healers assure us none of the women have the genetic signatures of a mate bond, and the male offspring are Kirenai."

A sense of unease filled Arazhi's stomach. "So what do you want me to do?"

"Go to Earth, find a willing female, and produce an heir. Quickly."

Arazhi took a step back. He'd pleasured his share of women, but never imagined doing so with the intent to produce a child. And he knew nothing about these humans. What if they really were as stupid as ijin'en? "How am I supposed to do that? Seduce my way across the planet until one of them gets pregnant?"

"Humans have agreed to hold an auction of willing females. Select one and do your duty. Now go. I must rest." His father's face disappeared beneath the surface, leaving behind only a ripple of green waves.

Arazhi turned to his damma. "He can't possibly be serious."

"He is." She once more took his hand, a worried smile on her pale face. "I've met a few of the captured human women, and they appear to make good mothers. Many insisted on remaining here on Kirenai Prime with their offspring. I've established a foundation to house them and help raise the children. My hope is that you find a female worthy of bonding while you are on Earth. Please say you'll at least try?"

"I shouldn't have to try." He scowled, thinking of those two years on Sireta Prime. "When I meet the right person, I'll just know."

"Shed your anger, Arazhi. Your heart has been closed for a long time. All I suggest is you open it again, or true happiness will never find you."

He swallowed and glanced at his father's pod. How was he supposed to pleasure a woman while his father might be dying? He rubbed his chin. "You think it was the Senburu who poisoned him?"

"That would make sense. They put forth a replacement, though his condition has not been made public."

"I'm going to track down who did this and punish them." He clenched his fists.

"We will. And the healers are doing their best to find an antidote for your father in the meantime. But right now, your job is to ensure our enemies can't seize power before we can finish the investigation, and the only way to do that is to produce an heir."

He sighed. He knew his duty. If humans were as willing to produce offspring as his father suggested, perhaps he wouldn't be gone long. Then he would see to the investigation himself and find revenge. "All right," he said. "I'll go to Earth and meet these humans."

3

*A*razhi's ship orbited the blue-green planet called Earth, waiting for his security officer, Zhiruto, to report back. The Intergalactic Dating Agency that had coordinated the auction charged exorbitant amounts to attend their events, which meant any other attendees would be either royalty or diplomats, like him, but after the attempt on the emperor's life, Zhiruto had insisted on checking the venue out first.

While he waited, Arazhi read over the list of cultural requirements the IDA had provided in their Earth orientation packet.

- Leashes required.
- Must be licensed and vaccinated.
- Feces must be cleaned up by owner.

- Control excessive barking.
- Fill in any holes created in lawn.
- No swimming in fountain.
- Do not interfere with wildlife.

Arazhi had been to many diverse planets and attended many interspecies functions, but leashes? Barking? Feces? What sort of race were these humans? No wonder his father had tried to keep the planet closed until the natives matured. Although Arazhi also couldn't deny that there was a certain appeal to the shape of the species' females now that he'd seen the images.

He practiced assuming the form of a human male once more, looking at himself via one of the camera feeds in his intergalactic vessel's living quarters. Human men seemed to prefer wearing long coverings for their legs and torsos, leaving only their hands and heads bare. Even their feet were covered, and he hadn't acquired any local clothing. Adjusting both color and shape wasn't easy, but he thought he'd done fairly well emulating long dark blue slacks and a blue collared shirt that matched his skin.

His communicator beeped, and Zhiruto's face took over the image on screen. "I've secured the area. All guests are accounted for. The universal translators are still updating hundreds of local languages, but it's safe for you to transport down, Prince Arazhi."

"All right, thank you." Arazhi didn't care for the transporter, preferring to land in the comfort and dignity of his ship, but non-essential technology was prohibited on newly introduced planets in order to keep it from ending up in the hands of natives who might not be ready for it.

He moved to the transport room and engaged the system. The computerized voice said, "Please prepare for deposition in aqueous habitat."

He hesitated. Humans were supposed to be land-based, but they hadn't yet formed a single language to share, so perhaps they hadn't yet settled on being land-based, either. And these were the same coordinates Zhiruto had used. He'd never learned to swim as a biped, and hated water-based landings in that form.

Releasing a breath, Arazhi relaxed into his amorphous resting state.

The familiar cold tingle of dematerialization swept through him, and his view of the transport bay blinked out. An instant later, he was surrounded by fresh, flowing water. Bright lights flickered from blue to red to purple below the surface, and below him, a tiled floor had been littered with metallic disks. No other beings appeared to be in the water.

He pulled himself into his human form, water running off his shoulders and down his sides. Once he'd fully coalesced into his upright shape, he looked around. The pool only reached his knees, and a jet of water spouted into the night air. A pounding beat of Earth music came from somewhere nearby, and several humans gaped at him from beneath strings of lights draped along a nearby concrete path. One pulled out a small device and began flashing a light at him. Was she signaling for him to approach?

He stepped over the edge of the pool toward them.

The humans were all female, wearing various colored gowns that showed a lot of brown or pink legs. They all held leads connecting them to small, furry quadrupeds. One quadruped was making a sharp, repetitive sound, its body jerking with each burst of noise. *Ah,* he thought. This explained the cultural requirement about leashes. The people on G'nax had a symbiotic relationship with an eight-legged insectoid. Did humans have quadruped symbiotes?

Before he could get close enough to ask, the females hurried away.

He didn't mind. It gave him a moment to smell the moist night air and watch a tiny insect with pale wings flutter against one of the lights. The path he stood on was edged with green vegetation, and he bent to touch the curiously even blades.

"My prince." A tall blue figure approached along the path from the direction of the music.

Although the form was unfamiliar, Arazhi recognized Zhiruto's Iki'i. His security officer had assumed the shape of a broadly muscled and bare-chested human, with thick blue hair falling in waves down his back. He carried a delicate flute of golden liquid in one hand.

"I was growing worried." Zhiruto said as he came to a halt. "Why didn't you use the updated coordinates I sent you?"

"I didn't receive them." Arazhi stood.

Zhiruto grimaced. "Sorry. The security systems have been getting some feedback and interfering with comm signals. I'll get that fixed right away."

Eyeing Zhiruto's half-clothed figure, Arazhi asked, "Do all males in this region dress like this?"

"No, but you know how I am with emulating clothing." Zhiruto winked. Clothing was the most difficult aspect Kirenai integrated into their shapeshifting. "And the females seem to like my current figure. Come, we don't want to miss the first bondservants up for auction."

They left the trail, cutting across the shorn blades toward a brightly lit dais where a band played. As they moved, Arazhi shifted again, emulating Zhiruto's easier-to-maintain form.

The band's melody was interesting, upbeat, reminding him of the balls he'd been to on Sireta Prime. At the base of the dais, several round tables hosted a smattering of Kirenai in human form, a pair of horned Khargals, and a single red-haired Fogarian with massive sideburns. Humans in black-and-white clothing moved between the tables carrying trays.

One of the female servers with brown hair pulled into a bun approached, carrying a tray filled with flutes of golden liquid. Her smile was nervous, but genuine. "Kan eek helf een?"

Arazhi frowned. "Excuse me?"

Zhiruto gestured toward the tray in the woman's hands. "She's offering you a drink."

He removed one of the flutes from her tray and nodded, taking note of her interest in Zhiruto's large muscles. He didn't even need to use his Iki'i to sense her attraction. She kept glancing over her shoulder toward them as she departed.

"You've garnered some attention, I see." Arazhi readjusted his musculature to more strongly resemble his security officer's.

"She's not one of the ones for sale," replied Zhiruto, pulling out a chair at a table in front of the stage. He was usually more interested in the females they met, but tonight he was all business. "The females we're after will be displayed for us there."

Arazhi looked toward the stage where several humans stood at the side, clustered around a female in a dark blue dress. His breath caught in his throat. The female's pale blonde hair was pulled up on top of her head, but tiny wisps had come loose along the sides, framing smooth rosy cheeks and glossed lips below a pair of glass lenses that accentuated her striking blue eyes. The neckline of her dress draped modestly over her collarbone, but left her shoulders and arms bare and did nothing to disguise her ample breasts and well-rounded hips.

She was stunning. But even more captivating was the way she directed the people around her.

He sighed and looked away. She was totally his type, but she wouldn't be one of the females for sale, not with a bearing like that. She was undoubtedly a princess or dignitary. If he was going to buy a slave, he'd do best to select the meekest one. A female who would have no designs on becoming queen once she bore his child and earned her freedom.

He sampled the carbonated liquid in his flute, recognized it as alcohol, and downed it in one swallow. At least these humans had good taste in beverages. As he was looking around for the woman with the tray, the lights went out, and a voice came over the speaker.

The words were garbled in his translator, but he caught enough to know the auction was about to begin.

On stage, a single spotlight popped to life, and the woman in the blue dress stepped into it. Once more, his breath caught in his throat.

She held a mic to her mouth. "Dang fur kom, ederon."

Her voice was like a song, and a shiver ran through him, as if a lover had just stroked his pleasure line. *Oritsu*, she was amazing. He stopped trying to decipher her words and simply allowed the cadence to float over him. Why couldn't she be for sale?

She handed the mic to a human male with a double chin and a patch of fur over his mouth who moved to a podium at the front of the stage. Lights popped on behind her, illuminating a cadre of females all dressed in gowns of sparkles and silk. Quite a few held animals in their arms or led them by leashes.

He leaned over to Zhiruto. "Are these creatures they carry symbiotic?"

"Not that I'm aware of." Zhiruto shrugged. "I believe they are for sale, too."

The quadrupeds were definitely gaining some interest from the Khargals, but not the kind he thought humans would appreciate. He nudged Zhiruto. "I get the sense these animals are precious to humans, not food. Go tell the Khargals before they try to eat one."

Zhiruto grumbled, but rose to speak with the gray-skinned aliens.

Arazhi settled back against his seat and watched the females parade across the stage in some sort of synchronized march, quadrupeds in tow. The music ended, and the women filed off stage. A tall woman with a sharp chin remained, and the man at the podium began chanting in a singsong voice.

The Fogarian at the next table raised a hand. "Eight thousand."

The double-chinned man pointed at him, and the woman nodded in his direction.

The auction has begun, Arazhi realized. He considered raising his hand, buying the woman, and getting this whole ordeal over with. Except he couldn't seem to take his eyes off the woman in blue standing at the edge of the stage. One after another, women appeared, were bought, and descended to meet their new owners. One after another, Arazhi couldn't bring himself to bid.

"Do none of these females entice you at all?" asked Zhiruto, who'd won a bid for a tall woman in a black dress.

Arazhi sighed and raised his hand to bid on the current offering, only to be outbid by the Fogarian.

Then the woman in the blue dress stepped forward once more, giving the audience a wide smile, one hand on her hip. His stomach sank. The auction was over, and he'd missed his chance. He glanced at the next table where a woman held a small quadruped on her lap and smiled nervously as the Kirenai reached out to stroke its fur.

At the podium, the auctioneer once more began his chant, and Arazhi's attention snapped back to the stage in disbelief.

The woman in the blue dress was for sale.

A Khargal raised his hand. "Nine thousand."

The woman smiled at him and made a small curtsey.

Arazhi was determined to have that smile all to himself. He raised his hand. "Ten."

The Khargal raised his hand again. "Fifteen."

This auction was pointless. Arazhi knew what he wanted, and money was no object, not when the fate of his dynasty was on the line. Plus, the mother of his child deserved recognition of her worth.

He rose from his seat. "Five hundred thousand."

The woman's eyes went round behind her lenses. She glanced at the auctioneer, who seemed just as stunned as she was.

The Khargal growled but crossed his arms and slumped back against his chair, shaking his head. "She's all yours, Kirenai."

For a moment, the entire world seemed to hold its breath.

Then the auctioneer banged his gavel. "Sold!"

And every human in the area burst into thunderous applause.

4

Georgie carefully made her way down the stage stairs, trying not to trip in the Louboutin stilettos she'd bought to go with her dress. She'd never owned shoes this expensive, not even for her wedding, but the Intergalactic Dating Agency had not only paid her up front for planning the event, it had reimbursed her for every receipt she submitted, including her formal wear. They seemed made of money, and she'd even secured stipends for her volunteers to buy gowns, which had made recruiting so easy, she'd eventually had to turn women away.

Every one of the aliens seemed to be rich, their bids escalating with every date auctioned. She almost wished she'd gone ahead and accepted every woman who'd volunteered. But that would be greedy. As it was, the shelter wouldn't need to worry about funding for the rest of its existence, especially with that final bid. *Five hundred thousand dollars!* And it had been for her.

Blinded by stage lights, she hadn't been able to see her bidder, but her date could have fins and fangs for all she cared. Heck, with the money they'd brought in, even Lora better not complain about this event, slime or no slime. Not that that was a worry. The aliens she'd glimpsed while coordinating the auction weren't bad to look at. A couple had horns, and she'd spotted one terrifying guy who reminded her of Arnold Schwartzenegger with fangs and a wild mop of crimson hair. But the rest just looked like humans with blue skin. Not scary at all.

Picking up a nearby bottle of champagne and an empty flute, she minced across the lawn toward his table, trying not to let her heels sink into the grass. Women sat with aliens at every table, some looking uncomfortable, others laughing or showing off pets. With the auction complete, it was time for the guests to get to know each other.

The alien who'd bid on Georgie was unmistakable as she wove between the tables toward him. His gaze remained fixed on her. She moved slowly, taking time to look him over. He was shirtless, and except for his blue skin and strangely dark eyes, he looked human. *Gorgeously human.* She gulped and forced a smile, wondering why he was shirtless. His broad shoulders and god-like chest and arms made it difficult for her to raise her attention to his face.

When she did, she was equally stunned. His square jaw was the epitome of handsome. Midnight blue eyes with no white seemed to bore directly through her. And a sensuous mouth smiled at her without actually turning upward, as if he knew a great secret only they shared.

She paused at the chair next to him and stuttered, "Thank you for your generosity. You've helped a lot of homeless pets." She lifted the bottle. "Shall we celebrate?"

He nodded and extended his empty champagne flute.

She filled it then her own before sitting down next to him.

He downed his in a single gulp, then resumed silently staring at her as the band began playing a popular Country Western song.

Her stomach fluttered. She downed her champagne, too, hoping it would calm her erratic nerves. She'd never expected an alien to be so handsome, much less seem to be interested in her.

The moment she set her glass down, he refilled it.

Strong silent types were definitely her thing, and everything about him had her mind going to naughty places. She hadn't been on a date since her divorce, so perhaps it was just easy for a man to turn her head, but to be fair, the guy had just dropped half a million dollars for a date with her and also looked yummier than any Chippendales model she'd ever seen.

Except this wasn't just any date, and he wasn't just any guy.

He was an alien. He might look human, but that didn't mean they were remotely compatible. Her gaze fluttered down toward his lap, suddenly wondering what alien peen might look like. Did he even have one?

She felt his smile on her, and heat crept up her cheeks again. Dragging her gaze back to his, she thrust out a hand. *At least learn his name first, girl.* "My name's Georgette, but everyone calls me Georgie." She had to half shout to be heard over the band. "What's yours?"

"Name," he said, as if feeling the word on his tongue. His voice was deep and smooth—another of her weaknesses. "Arazhi," he rumbled.

She gulped. "Good to meet you, Arazhi."

He looked like he wanted to lick her all over as he reached out and took her offered hand. The contact sent a jolt of awareness through her, and she immediately recalled Lora's quip about doing more than making friends on a first date. Georgie tended to be more reserved, but for this guy…

Gripping her hand gently, he lifted it toward his mouth as if to kiss it. But instead of a kiss, his tongue flicked out along the slit between her index and middle finger, dipping in at the apex in a way that totally had her thinking of other slits. Was this how aliens greeted each other? Her panties felt suddenly wet.

"Oh, my," she whispered, voice drowned out by the roll of the auctioneer. She clenched her thighs together and glanced around, worried someone might somehow notice how turned on she was, but everyone's attention was elsewhere.

All attention except Arazhi's. His thumb traced the trail his tongue had left, sending another shiver straight to her core.

She laughed uncomfortably and pulled her hand away, picking up her champagne. She really shouldn't drink more, not when she hadn't eaten all day. The alcohol was going to her head. That had to be why her body was responding this way. Her heart raced and her skin felt flushed.

There were supposed to be hors d'oeuvres at the event, but she hadn't noticed any pass their way. Where the hell were the servers? She glanced around for one, but there were none in sight.

She set the glass on the table and stood. "I need to go check on something."

Arazhi stood with her, putting a hand on her elbow. "Hungry."

She wasn't sure if he was saying he was hungry, or somehow sensing she was, but all the guests were likely feeling peckish by now. Hangry aliens were the last thing she needed. "I'll be right back with food."

But her alien apparently didn't understand he didn't need to tag along and trailed her between the tables toward the caterer's tent. She found a harried looking woman in a white caterer's jacket opening more champagne. "Why isn't there any food out there?" Georgie demanded.

The woman wrinkled her nose. "We served the early arrivals, but those aliens with horns ate everything we had ten minutes after they'd arrived."

Crap. Georgie glanced through the darkness toward the table in question. A horned, gray-skinned alien had apparently won the bid for Maise, who now sat between him and another like him, clutching her dog against her chest as if worried they thought it was the main course.

"Why didn't anyone tell me?" Georgie glowered at the caterer. This was exactly why her being in the auction had been a bad idea. She needed to be available to make sure everything ran smoothly. "Send one of your people out to pick up cheese and vegetable trays or something. Put it on my account. I have a feeling these aliens aren't picky."

"Yes, miss. Right away." The caterer rushed off to do as instructed.

Georgie turned to find Arazhi grinning at her, once more looking like he knew a secret. He had a dimple on one cheek. God, she was a sucker for dimples. Was it possible for him to get any sexier? She swallowed and smiled back.

"Come," he said, and once more took her elbow, guiding her away from the auction toward the park.

"I really shouldn't leave." She looked over her shoulder toward the stage where another auctioned woman in gold sequins was holding up her cat like Rafiki in *The Lion King*.

Arazhi's hand remained firmly on her elbow, propelling her toward the fountain. "Please, keep talking."

What a strange request. "About what?"

He tapped a finger to his ear. "Translator is learning."

"Oh." She hadn't even given a second thought to whether or not aliens spoke English. *Shit, what if he didn't know how much he'd actually bid?* Wouldn't it be just her luck to learn the aliens were spending their version of Monopoly money? "Have you understood what's going on tonight?"

He stopped and turned her to face him, his dimple once more in place. "Money is good."

She was relieved to hear it. Still, she pretended to wave away her concern. "Oh, I wasn't worried about that. I just want to make sure you're having a good time."

He stepped closer, forcing her to look up.

She inhaled a nervous breath. He smelled amazing, slightly sweet and a bit like good tobacco.

With one hand, he brushed a tendril of hair from her face, looking down into her eyes with a fierce possessiveness that made her legs feel like jelly. His baritone voice repeated, "Good time."

Is he going to kiss me?

Even as she thought it, one powerful arm circled her waist, pulling her against him.

Her nipples tightened, and the place between her thighs pulsed with need. He was warm, hard muscles to her soft curves. She let her head fall back, closing her eyes.

The explosion of sensation when his lips met hers left her dizzy. It was as if unadulterated desire poured into her bloodstream. His kiss was soft yet firm, his tongue sliding hotly between her lips like ambrosia filling her mouth. He plundered her for what felt like an eternity, yet ended too soon. His big hand splayed at the small of her back, keeping her pressed against what was very obviously a throbbing erection.

At the edge of her awareness, sounds penetrated her fog of desire. A dog was yipping. Something crashed. Screams filled the air.

Jolted from the dream-like kiss, she pushed off Arazhi's chest. Something was wrong.

Several party guests ran past her toward the parking lot.

She grabbed the arm of one woman who ran past. "What's happening?"

"The aliens are shooting death rays or something! A bunch of them dissolved into goo!" The woman jerked away and kept running.

"Oh, God!" This was not a contingency she'd planned for. *What should I do?* She hiked up her dress and kicked off her shoes, preparing to go back and stop the chaos.

The blue alien who'd been sitting next to Arazhi ran toward them, shouting something.

Behind her, Arazhi said, "Danger."

Before she took another step, he jerked her back against his chest.

"Put me down!" She struggled. "I have to stop this!"

But his grip was like an iron band. Then, it was as if she was suddenly encased in shrink wrap. Everything went blurry. She couldn't move, couldn't breathe. The ground seemed to wobble and shift.

And she was no longer standing in the park.

5

Arazhi's security officer wasn't one to exaggerate danger, so when Zhiruto shouted for the prince to transport off the planet, Arazhi'd quickly encased Georgie within his matrix and signaled his ship for pickup. Not the most elegant way to get her on board his vessel, but his transporter didn't yet have her genetic signature, and he wasn't about to leave her behind.

They rematerialized on the bridge, and Georgie stumbled forward, gasping. His Iki'i picked up on her shock, which was understandable; she came from a primitive species after all. She likely had no idea where they were or how they'd arrived.

While she stood with her back to him, gaping at the view screen displaying a portion of Earth's blue-green horizon, he reassembled his matrix into the human form she preferred. He'd been making slight adjustments to his features all night and believed he'd achieved her standard of attractive. The next step would be assessing her likes and dislikes when it came to the more personal aspects of his anatomy.

He moved to the communication console. He needed to find out what had happened on Earth. Where was Zhiruto? His security officer should've arrived on deck right behind him.

"Zhiruto, are you still planet-side?"

A familiar blue face appeared on screen. "Yes. I've ordered all transporters blocked to prevent suspects from escaping."

"Do you think someone was trying to assassinate me?"

"We must assume so." A dog was barking, and the image canted sideways as Zhiruto glanced over his shoulder toward a woman in a crimson gown restraining a gangly, russet-furred quadruped.

Georgie pushed up beside Arazhi, placing her fingers against the screen. "Lora! Aryou kay?"

The universal translator seemed to be catching up, but still wasn't perfect. The woman in the uniform turned to face the camera, looking over Zhiruto's shoulder. "Georgie? Where are you?"

The screen resumed its focus on Zhiruto. "My prince, you must leave orbit immediately. I don't know how many assassins there are or if any escaped back to their ships before the shutdown. You could still be in danger."

"I'm not leaving without you." Leaving his security officer behind was a huge breach of protocol, not to mention Zhiruto was his friend.

"I'm going to keep searching here. I'll be fine, but you cannot be compromised. Now go!"

Arazhi hesitated, then hit the button that would execute the pre-programmed escape route. He hated leaving Zhiruto behind, but he trusted his security officer knew what he was doing.

A small shudder preceded the change of trajectory, then the view screen went black as they entered FTL.

Georgie grabbed his arm. "Call them back. I need to know if my friends are okay."

Putting a hand gently on her shoulder, he transmitted calm. "Communication is impossible while the Faster Than Light drive is active, but my security officer has everything in hand. Don't worry. We'll find out more after we reach Kirenai Prime."

"K-kirenai Prime? What's that?"

"My home planet."

"The hell?" She shrugged off his grasp. "I'm not going to another planet. I need to get back to Earth! Turn us around right now."

He sensed that she was focusing on her responsibilities in order to keep her mounting panic at bay. Staying in control made her feel secure. *She is going to be an impressive mother to our children*, he thought. He smiled and radiated pleasure, anticipation, and an innuendo of desire. He couldn't help the last part. Something about her made him want—need—to make her happy. Though she'd sold herself as a bondservant, he planned to treat her like a princess. "We can't stop until we reach our destination. Come. We will eat now."

She took a step back. "I don't want to eat. I want off this ship. Take me back to Earth this instant."

Now her stubbornness was becoming a nuisance. It was her job to make him happy, not the other way around. He set his jaw and wrapped one hand around her elbow to guide her from the bridge. "Your responsibility is only to me from now on."

"What are you talking about?"

He frowned. Why did she continue to radiate confusion? She'd come to his table after he'd purchased her contract. "I purchased your contract. You belong to me now."

She gasped and stumbled, even though she no longer wore those ridiculous pointy shoes. "You thought you were buying a slave?"

He blinked. "Of course."

Her mouth dropped open. "It was a charity auction, for God's sake! A benefit for our animal shelter. You bought a *date* with me, not a lifetime of servitude."

He narrowed his eyes. He'd spent an exorbitant amount on her, and while money wasn't the issue, he wasn't about to let things go. She was perfect, and he wanted her more than he'd ever desired a female before. "Earth was only allowed to join the consortium because they offered us willing females. Did you not accept my bid?"

"Well, yes, but—"

"Then, as a royal bondservant, you'll be treated well. I'll even grant you freedom after we successfully breed."

A spike of arousal wafted from her, at odds with the sharp tone of her voice. "Breed? As in make babies?"

"Yes. I require a male child."

She laughed harshly. "Well, joke's on you, buddy. You won't be getting a kid out of me, male or otherwise."

He tilted his head. Georgie's emotions were a whirlwind of contradictions through his Iki'i. She wanted to be with him and seemed to desire a child. But she also resisted her desires. "I'm offering you great pleasure."

Her lips parted a moment, and she exhaled slowly before saying, "If you truly want to please me, take me home."

Perhaps he was being too soft with her. Little was known about human mating habits, but many species required an interested male to press his advance until the female relented. Taking her shoulders, he backed her toward the lavender wall. "You'll enjoy our breeding, I promise."

Sexual energy flowed like a current between them. She did enjoy his forcefulness. Yet still she protested. "You don't understand. This factory's out of order. Condemned."

He didn't understand her idiom. *The universal translator must still be updating,* he thought. But language didn't always require words.

Running his hands down her arms, he inserted his thumbs between her fingers the way she'd liked at the party. Her blue eyes had darkened, and her cheeks were flushed as pink as the sun on Hynodae. Dipping his head, he brushed her soft lips with his.

She sucked in a startled breath, body perfectly still.

Hovering a breath away, he opened his Iki'i, searching for her true desire. Bondservant or no, he wouldn't breed with an unwilling female. There was something in her emotions he didn't understand, a fear of something other than him. But even stronger was the sense that she enjoyed his mouth on hers.

He lifted one hand to her throat, tilting her face toward him. He slid his tongue along her parted lips, gently exploring the contours. She put her palms against his chest, as if intending to push him away. But she didn't try to move him. Instead, her fingers slid across his pecs, exploring the muscles he'd created.

A brief flicker of gratitude that he'd followed Zhiruto's lead in choosing a form ran through him, then his tongue was pressing inside her mouth. Her lips softened and opened further, accepting his slow, questioning strokes. He delved deeper, his Iki'i thrilling with her rising desire.

She tasted like morning dew on happa fronds, slightly sweet with a hint of musk. No wonder the black market was abducting human females. Were they all this intoxicating? He didn't think so. He hadn't felt remotely attracted to the other women he'd seen at the auction.

The only one he wanted was Georgie.

He palmed her waist, loving the curve while at the same time imagining his child swelling within her. Never in all his experience had a woman made him think like this. Made him feel so right inside his skin. Georgie was special. He'd been right about his first assessment of her—she wasn't meant to be a bondservant, and he wouldn't enforce her contract.

But he was going to convince her to be his lover.

Making a baby had been a fantasy of Georgie's for as long as she'd known about sex—a fantasy that had been ground to dust by years of fertility treatments, with the remaining particles blown away by her divorce. There would never be a baby for her. Yet Arazhi's talk about breeding swept through her like a drug.

He prodded his tongue between her teeth, muscular chest pressing her against the curved alien wall behind her. A tingle of desire raced from her nipples to her center. She wasn't small or dainty, but the way his body covered hers, the way his big hand cradled her head as he kissed her, made her feel more feminine than she'd ever felt before. Like she was made for kissing.

His kissing.

She raised her chin to meet him, sliding her hands up his bare chest to explore his muscles. He was ripped, without an ounce of fat on his body, and the fact that he wanted her was mind-boggling. He obviously didn't understand that she couldn't bear him a child, but she'd been honest, so for now, she was going to enjoy the pleasure he'd promised. It wasn't as if she could do anything to help her friends from here, anyway.

His palm slid up her waist until his thumb stopped at the crease below one of her breasts.

Nipples aching for his touch, she arched her back.

He cupped her breast, thrusting his tongue into her mouth with quick, sure strokes.

She couldn't remember the last time she'd been so thoroughly kissed. It was making her dizzy. Her hands slid around the solid muscles along his ribs as if he was the only thing holding her upright.

His thumb stroked over the fabric covering her nipple, making it harden in response. She could only imagine how much better it would feel on her bare skin.

As if of the same thought, he slid the spaghetti strap of her gown off her shoulder and down her arm, exposing the top of her strapless bra.

She tilted her head, letting his questing tongue lave her skin. Shudders of delight coursed through her at his touch. She hadn't been with a man since Josh had left her, and her hormones were on fire.

Arazhi tugged the strap, breaking it in half, and she snapped back to reality. This gown had cost a fortune. She grabbed his hand. "What are you doing? Don't rip my dress."

Arazhi stepped back so quickly she nearly collapsed. His eyes were wide as he looked at the broken shoulder strap. "Have I harmed you?"

She held the severed edge of the strap, trying to determine if it could be repaired. "You could've used the zipper."

"What is a zipper?"

She let out a slow breath and bit her bottom lip. He didn't know what a zipper was. *He's an alien, what did you expect?* She shouldn't be making out with him, anyway. She had to focus on getting home. Swallowing, she smoothed one hand up the front of the gown to cover her exposed bra. "How long until we reach your planet?"

"Approximately sixteen jiros."

She really hoped jiros translated to minutes. "Uh, can you give me that in Earth time?"

"I believe it is almost two of your Earth days."

Her stomach cramped. *Two days?* Double that if she counted the return trip. And she still had no idea if her friends were okay. "Can we go any faster?"

"Not appreciably, no." He tilted his head, as if listening to something. "You are hungry. Come, I will show you the galley." Without waiting for her to agree, he turned and exited the room.

She was hungry, and if she was about to face multiple days of space travel, she should probably eat. As she followed Arazhi, she glanced at the strange pastel walls around her, nervous about what aliens might consider food. She'd seen several episodes of Star Trek where aliens ate live worms or other gross items.

Reality suddenly hit her—she was on an alien spaceship. And everything was completely different from anything she'd ever imagined. The walls weren't metal, but ribbed like giant leaves and glowing with pale lavender light, like something out of a fairy story. The air smelled sweet and slightly like wintergreen, with a warm current of fresh air flowing from the curved hall Arazhi had entered.

She ran her fingertips along a thick support rib running the length of the hall. The surface felt warm and leathery, almost alive. "What is this wall made of?"

"The interior walls are grown from a variant of popotan." He looked over his shoulder at her, his dimple flirting with the edge of his almost smile. "I look forward to showing you the farms where we grow it on Kirenai Prime. The rolling hills there are lovely."

She dropped her hand from the wall and glared at him. "We will not be going on a field trip to some farm. The moment we reach your planet, we're going to contact the IDA and straighten this out."

"Of course." He returned his attention to the hallway ahead. "I'm simply saying you would find the farms enjoyable. I used to play there as a child."

Her footsteps slowed. She was trying to be angry with him, to resist the lure of a dream that could never come true. But what if his species had technology that would allow her to bear a child? *A tiny Arazhi would be so cute,* she thought, picturing a chubby blue toddler playing among rows of purple leaves. *And making that baby with Arazhi...* Her insides tingled with the memory of his hand on her breast.

She let her gaze follow the muscular curve of his blue shoulder to the planes of his back. Alien or not, he pushed all the right buttons for her. Tall, deep-voiced, muscular, and that dimple when he smiled—she was continually on the verge of forgetting everything and letting him pleasure her like he promised.

She shook her head, refusing to follow her thoughts. Arazhi wasn't asking to marry her and have a family.

He wanted to *breed* her as if she was livestock. He'd even said he'd grant her freedom afterward, which could only mean he intended to take the child from her. No way was she going to have a baby only to give it up. But leaving Earth to live on an alien planet? No way. She had parents, friends, and a life—such as it was.

Arazhi entered a door to the left, and she paused at the threshold. Storage shelves were inset between the ribs in the walls here, and a brushed gold table rested in the center, surrounded by plush violet captain's chairs. A heavenly scent reached her, reminding her of roast pork with apples as Arazhi set an oval platter on the table.

Her stomach growled, and she looked at the orange glistening lumps sitting on top of something that might pass for rice. Despite her growing hunger, her concern about eating alien food returned. "Are you sure humans can eat your food?"

He smiled, his dimple once more making her insides flutter. "I verified that everything here is compatible with human physiology." He set a basket of round red fruits that looked like plums with pointed ends next to the platter. "Let me show you how we eat this dish."

Transferring a fruit to a shallow bowl, he deftly squished it into a paste with a utensil that looked like a small spatula. He turned the spatula around and poked the pointed end of the handle into one of the orange lumps, dipped it into the paste, then returned the paste-covered morsel to the platter where he rolled it around to pick up the pale brown grain.

Holding it toward her mouth, he said, "Try it."

Jaw tight, she shook her head. "You first."

He laughed and ate it, then repeated the process, offering the next bite to her. "You may spit it out if you find it distasteful."

The food smelled edible, and he seemed to enjoy it. And she would have to eat something before they got back to Earth. Might as well do it now. She opened her mouth and let him place the food on her tongue.

An explosion of flavor filled her senses—sweet and rich with a hint of spice. It was crunchy on the outside and soft and juicy on the inside, somewhat like fried chicken. The delicious flavor flowed down her throat before she could even think to stop it. "What is this? It's amazing."

"A dish called akeno. It's a root with a glaze of urebi, one of my favorites."

"I can see why." She reached for the other spatula utensil, but he already had another bite up to her mouth.

This time she took the utensil from him to feed herself, relishing the flood of flavor. As she finished chewing, he slid a cup in her direction. "This pairs well. Try it."

She sniffed the bubbly liquid. It smelled like alcoholic Sweet Tarts. She took a tiny sip. The hint of sour was a perfect complement to the akeno, and she took a bigger drink. "This is refreshing. Thank you."

"We make it from zhupakuri fruit. It's native to Kirenai Prime."

Relaxing into her chair, she let him feed her another bite. She hated to admit it, but she could get used to treatment like this. "What do your species call themselves? Kirenai?"

He beamed at her. "Correct."

Damn. Why did she like his smile so much? She took another sip to hide her distraction. "Why did you leave your friend behind?" She hadn't understood their language, but she'd sensed the tension between them during the call earlier. "The people that ran past us near the fountain said something about aliens turning into puddles of goo."

Arazhi's eyes flashed, and he sat up straighter. "You mean they destabilized?" Before she could answer, he rose, his face a grimace of anger. "*Kuzara*, the food."

Georgie put a hand over her mouth as she remembered how quickly the hors d'oeuvres had been eaten. "Oh, God, I never imagined our food might be harmful to aliens."

"Human food is not harmful to us. The IDA verified compatibility before the party."

She let out a shaky breath. "Then what do you mean?"

He paced to the other side of the room and back. "It was an assassination attempt. Someone poisoned the emperor the same way. Now they're after me."

"You? Why?"

He paused his pacing. "I'm his sole heir."

She gulped as the implication sank in. If Arazhi was the son of an emperor, that could mean only one thing.

She'd been purchased by a prince.

*A*razhi stood still, watching Georgie's expression shift as her roving emotions teased his Iki'i. Women always fell all over him the moment they learned who he was, and he expected no different from this gorgeous Earth woman.

But when she met his eyes she asked, "Is your father all right?"

Her sincere compassion sliced straight to his heart. He was used to doling out empathy, not receiving it. All the anxiety he'd bottled up since learning of his father's condition threatened to break loose. "I don't know," he said, keeping his voice even. "Our healers were still looking for an antidote when I left."

"I'm sorry." Georgie knitted her brows. "Are you two not close?"

"Why would you ask that?" He frowned, affronted by her question. Family meant everything to Kirenai; from the moment they bonded, they lived and died for mate and children. Kirenai children honored and cherished their parents. "Of course we're close. He's my father."

She shrank back in her seat, embarrassment wafting toward him. "It's just that you're here, not with him. If it was my father, I'd want to be with him every moment to make sure he was all right."

He grimaced, suddenly realizing his hands were balled into fists. He didn't want to frighten her. Relaxing his posture, he returned to his seat in the chair next to her. Perhaps if she understood the true reason he needed her, she would stop resisting. "We are close. But if I don't produce an heir before he dies, my family will lose the throne."

"Oh." Her brow furrowed. "Why come all the way to Earth? Don't you have any women on your planet?"

This conversation was taking an unexpected turn, and he didn't feel like getting into a biology lesson about shapeshifting and pair bonding right now, so he kept things simple. "Kirenai require a female of a different species to reproduce. Humans are reported to be the most prolific, and I need a female who can conceive and bear a child quickly."

Her body tensed, and she shook her head. "I don't know any women who'd be willing to have a baby and just hand it over like that, especially to someone who lives on another planet. Visitation rights would be a nightmare."

"I wouldn't dream of separating a mother from her child. Part of the reason I came to Earth was that I was told humans make excellent mothers."

"Oh." She looked away. Regret floated like a sour miasma around her. "In that case, I'm sure you can find a woman willing to have your baby as soon as we get back to Earth. There were quite a few volunteers for the auction who I had to turn away."

He frowned. He thought he'd been paying her a compliment, assuring her he trusted her to become a mother to his child. Why did she continue to deny her own desire? Was this trait unique to Georgie, or were all human females this difficult? He placed a gentle hand on her arm. "But I don't want another female. I want you."

She shoved away from the table and stood, regret now consumed by searing hurt and anger. "You aren't listening to me. Unless you have a way to fix broken hardware, you need to find someone else to make alien babies with, okay?"

Again with the undecipherable idioms. "I don't understand."

Her eyes glistened as she pointed to her stomach. "I'm barren. Infertile. Broken. Defective." Her voice cracked. "Unable to have children. Understand?"

He didn't need to use his Iki'i to feel her pain. He could see it in her eyes. "Ah." He shifted his gaze to her middle. "Is it physical or genetic?"

"I don't know!" She turned away. "The doctors ran every test they could and couldn't fix me. Just take me back to Earth and swap me out. I'm sure an alien prince as hot as you are won't have any trouble finding someone else."

Pain and angst welled over him in waves, filling the room like the bitter scent of nilgawood resin. All he wanted was to soothe her. "Human physiology is new to the galactic consortium, but there are healers among the Qalqan who—"

She sliced a hand through the air. "I tried to have a baby for eight years, and I'm done with heartbreak. I can't handle another failure. Besides, you don't have time for tests and treatments. You need someone to pop out a kid quick."

Then he understood—she wasn't resisting him so much as she wanted to do the right thing. She was being honest. But her sincerity only made him want her more. "You let me worry about that."

Hope flared against his Iki'i, but died almost as quick. "Worry all you want, but leave me out of it. I've moved on."

He could tell she hadn't moved on; she still yearned for exactly what he was offering, regardless of her refusal to see a healer. And he wanted her regardless of her capacity to bear children, even if only for a single interlude of passion. "Then let's not talk about it anymore. I'd still like to give you pleasure if you're willing. We won't reach Earth again for several of your days, and I can think of no better way to spend that time."

She squeezed her eyes closed, wiping angrily at a tear that escaped one corner.

It wasn't a yes, but it wasn't a no, either, and he could sense she was tempted. He stood to face her and gently tucked a strand of hair behind her ear, letting his fingertips trail lightly down the side of her neck to her shoulder. Her indecision felt like a sheet of brittle ice melting in the sun. He leaned closer, letting his breath heat the skin where his fingers had touched. "What do you have to lose?"

Biting her bottom lip, she shrugged. "I guess I've got nothing better to do." She lifted red-rimmed eyes to meet his. "As long as you understand there'll be no babies."

He smiled and pulled her into his arms. "Think only of pleasure."

He was going to make her forget all about pain and regret.

oward the end of Georgie's marriage, sex had become so focused on getting her pregnant, it had felt like a chore. Arazhi was offering her a chance to enjoy her own body again. And it had been so long since she'd felt desirable.

She relaxed into his arms, still worried she was making a mistake. She could enjoy being with him now, before he moved on and found a suitable woman. One who could give him everything she couldn't. She'd been relieved to learn he didn't intend to take his child from its mother, but it was a bittersweet relief. *Why can't it be me?*

Arazhi kissed her softly, as if sensing her need for tenderness, stroking her hair, feathering butterfly kisses over her cheeks and eyelids. Then he pressed his forehead to hers, just holding her and letting his presence wash over her.

After a few calm moments, he said, "Come."

Taking her hand, he led her down the purple-veined hallway to another curved room. A circular bed made up with sheets that looked like iridescent mirror glaze sat in the center. Shelves lined the walls, filled with an assortment of odd items. Her gaze snagged on a flickering cube with the image of a blue man with his arm around an alabaster-skinned woman. Arazhi's parents? But before she could ask, she was pushed back onto the bed.

The shimmering covers felt buttery soft against her bare arms and shoulders. All thoughts of his family photos left her as she looked up at the perfectly cut muscles of Arazhi's torso and abs. His midnight dark eyes were sexy as hell, and the way he was looking at her made her breath catch in her throat.

He placed his hands on her thighs and slowly slid up her gown, letting the air caress her legs. By the time the hem reached the top of her thighs, her entire body trembled with anticipation. He let his thumbs slide between her legs, stroking softly upward in exactly the way she'd imagined when he'd licked between her fingers.

She let out a shaky breath and relaxed her legs, letting them part beneath his touch as he worked his way up. His fingertip bumped against her panties, and she flexed toward him involuntarily.

Chuckling, he ran his thumbs over the lace covering her hips, sending shivers of delight straight to her core.

"I want to see you naked," he said. "Show me how to remove your gown."

Although she felt ready to rip her panties off and let him take her, she complied and rolled over onto her stomach. "Pull down on the metal tab."

His knees sank into the mattress on either side of her as he straddled her hips, then the warmth of his hands met her back. He lowered the zipper until it stopped at the base of her spine. "Intriguing closure."

She chuckled. "I thought you were an advanced species. How can you be unfamiliar with a zipper?"

"We use *supo* cloth. No need for zippers." His hands slid along her back beneath the bodice and over the strap of her bra, easily discovering how to release the constricting elastic. With a deft pull, he detangled her from the gown and flipped her onto her back once more, leaving her in nothing but her panties.

He licked his lips, hungry gaze roaming her body.

She breathed shallowly, letting her own attention run down his gorgeous body. Her eyes widened at the sight of his bulging crotch. She swore she could see the actual outline of his dick beneath his pants. Heat flooded her panties. What did he look like?

She sat up and reached for his waistband. "I want to see you, too."

He took her hands in his, stopping her. "Do not be alarmed."

His words made her gulp, eyes locked on his bulge. "I wasn't until you said something."

Whatever was under his clothes was pulsing—actually pulsing. She was about to see an alien cock. What if he was too big for her? Or shaped strange? She didn't mind a little kink, but just how kinky was this about to get? Were they even compatible?

Then, right before her eyes, his pants seemed to melt away, and she was looking at a thick blue shaft between heavily muscled legs. It looked like her favorite vibrator, a pronounced head with ridges along the top of the shaft and a clit tickler at the base—except this piece of masculinity was very much alive. A small bead of pre-cum glistened at the tip.

She gasped and raised her eyes to his. "Your pants were an illusion?"

He laughed. "I guess you might say that."

She ran one finger along the top of his curved length. His skin was hot, and he grunted softly at her touch, thrusting his hips forward. She leaned in, inhaling his clean masculinity. She'd never wanted to taste a man like she wanted to taste him. Circling her tongue over the turgid head, she wrapped one hand around the base of his shaft. His taste was rich with a hint of spice that was potently male.

He remained perfectly still as she explored. Mouth opening wide, she took him in deeper. As her fingers circled his dick, she felt another protrusion below his shaft, between his ball sack and dick. Her pussy clenched, imagining what that might be for.

Flattening her tongue against the sensitive underside, she sucked in her cheeks and drew back.

He groaned, a low, deep sound that sent heat straight to her pussy and spread up her abdomen to her nipples.

She took him in again until his cock bumped the back of her throat. He was the perfect length, thick and solid.

His fingers released her hair from its messy bun, threading through the strands as she worked his shaft, losing herself in his flavor and heat.

Suddenly, he pulled away, urging her backward onto the soft iridescent sheets. He slid a knee between her legs, spreading them under his hungry touch.

Her nipples were rock hard, and wetness soaked her panties. His breath fanned over her inner thighs as he pulled her panties from her, then kissed his way up the inside of her legs to her center. He pushed a finger inside her, his tongue circling her clit as he drew out, then thrust back in. Out. In. Long thick finger driving in until his knuckles met her outer lips, hot tongue flicking over her clit. Her juices coated her thighs.

An orgasm rose inside her, hot and tight, and she bucked her hips in time to his plunging finger. She couldn't remember ever needing to come this fast. As she strained to reach the crest, he pushed in hard, and she felt a firm probing at her back hole. Before she could clench, he'd entered her there.

She screamed as the wave broke, pleasure shuddering through her as he continued plunging in and out with both fingers.

When she came down enough to regain her senses, he crawled up her body, sucking in one nipple, then the other. "Are you ready for me, Georgie?"

"Yes," she gasped. She needed more of him. Needed to be filled completely.

He settled between her legs, thick cock pressing her entrance. It stretched her opening almost to the point of pain. But he didn't hurt her. Pushing in shallowly, he locked eyes with her, rocking in and out, sinking deeper. Deeper. She could feel every ridge along his shaft as he entered.

When his hips met hers, he let out a long sigh. "So hot."

She panted against his shoulder, hands clawing his back. That part of him she'd thought was a clit tickler did exactly that, cupping and kneading her swollen bud and making her squirm with pleasure. The smaller protrusion below his main shaft prodded her ass without entering, which was good. His cock alone was huge, and she wasn't sure she could take more of him inside her.

He eased back, tilting his hips in such a way that kept his tickler on just the right spot, then thrust in again. She gasped, bucking in time to his increasing rhythm. As her muscles spasmed, she tossed her head against the covers. Her hands clutched his shoulders. All she could do was hang on as ecstasy flooded her.

He drove forward, hips slamming into hers. Heat exploded against her inner walls, and he grunted.

Riding out her own wave, she managed to crack her eyes open and watch his abs flex as he continued to pulse inside her. He was staring at her, his intensity sexy enough to make her orgasm flutter once more.

When she could breathe again, he lowered himself on top of her and murmured into her neck. "Next time will be even better. I promise."

She couldn't imagine better. Her body felt like a giant marshmallow floating in a sea of hot chocolate. But hell if she was going to say no to a next time.

They made love several more times before Georgie could no longer stay awake. She'd never lost herself so deeply to any experience. Her brain was in a heavy fog as she lay on her side with Arazhi's body curled around hers. She was surprised by how safe she felt as she drifted to sleep.

She didn't know how much time had passed when she opened her eyes and stretched to find herself alone. Her heart constricted. She'd hoped to find Arazhi next to her, smiling with that sweet dimple. To spend a few lazy hours in his bed, talking and getting to know him. But that wasn't what he'd promised. He'd offered her a mere few hours of pleasure, nothing more. Now she'd return to Earth, and he'd find a woman who could provide what he wanted—a baby.

Get over it, Georgie, she told herself. She wasn't meant to be a mother, and she barely knew Arazhi, anyway. When she got home, she'd see what she could salvage of her wrecked event planning business, get out of her parents' apartment, maybe adopt a dog, and get on with her life—assuming the chaos with the poisoned aliens hadn't caused the end of the world.

Thinking about Earth again got her blood flowing, and she once more worried about her friends. No longer wanting sleep, she reached for the floor near the bed, searching for her glasses. She didn't remember taking them off, and hoped they hadn't gotten crushed. Thankfully, they were fine, folded neatly and waiting for her by the bed on a low table she hadn't noticed earlier. She settled them on her nose and spotted her dress hanging against the opposite wall. She would've liked to wear something more comfortable, but none of the shelves held clothing, only the curios and image cubes she'd noted earlier.

Rising, she went over and pulled down the garment. The strap had been repaired as if by magic, with no sign of damage. Arazhi's ship must have some sort of fabric repair technology she wasn't aware of. That had been nice of him, at least. A parting gift before he sent her on her way. Her bra and panties lay folded on the shelf nearby.

She stepped into her dress while examining a nearby cube with flickering images. In one photo, a blue-skinned man stood between two aliens with green and yellow scales. He bore a slight resemblance to Arazhi, but she couldn't be sure if it was him or a close relative. The next image was a different blue-skinned man with his arm around a short woman with alabaster skin and dark blue hair. The woman wore a crown that looked like it was made of interwoven diamonds and gazed at the man with obvious adoration. *Arazhi's parents?*

The image shifted to a short video of the same woman, only without a crown this time, bouncing a small blue toddler while the blue man watched with obvious love in his gaze. Double moons hovered over rolling purple hills in the background. *That must be a young Arazhi and his parents visiting the fields he mentioned.* Georgie's chest tightened at the thought of Arazhi taking his new family on a trip, his dark eyes filled with love as he watched over the mother of his child.

Enough torturing myself. Turning away, she went to the lavatory and cleaned herself up. At least a lavatory was a lavatory, even on an alien ship. When she returned, soft music was playing, and a small table and two chairs had appeared in the room. A rich, buttery smell with hints of fruit wafted from a covered plate on the table.

Arazhi entered carrying two glasses. He set them on the table. "I was hungry and thought you might be, as well. Please, sit."

A wave of giddiness passed through her. *He didn't just use and abandon me.* Or even leave a servant to see to her. He'd come back to take care of her himself. Suddenly ravenous, she gladly took the seat beside him, wondering what alien delicacy he had for her today.

He lifted the lid, exposing what looked like sticky buns. "Baked *kazhitu.* A type of nut that grows on my mother's planet." He picked one up with his fingers and put it on a small plate in front of her. "I believe you will like it."

There were no utensils in sight, so Georgie picked up a bun with her fingers. She took a small nibble, surprised by how soft it was as it all but melted on her tongue. The sticky glaze tasted like apple pie filling. "Oh, wow."

Arazhi smiled and took one himself, devouring half in a single bite. He poured them each a large glass of what looked like orange juice and took a deep gulp.

Cautious about chasing the sticky bun sweetness with sour juice, Georgie took a cautious sip. A flavor like sweet cream, only cleaner and more refreshing, hit her tongue. She took a bigger drink, realizing how parched she was. Not surprising, considering how active she'd been for the last few hours. Heat crept into her cheeks at the memory.

A warm hand covered her thigh, sending a jolt of awareness straight to her tired pussy. She looked up, startled. Arazhi's midnight eyes made her want to fall into them and never come out.

"You're very sexy when you enjoy your food, *kikajiru*," he murmured.

The heat in her cheeks intensified. "Uh, thanks." Why was he still trying to charm her? She'd been very clear about their situation. She was tempted to set him straight again, but another part of her just wanted to enjoy being pampered. "What does *kikajiru* mean?"

"Distracting one."

Unsure if that was a compliment or not, she changed the subject, pointing toward the picture cube she'd looked at earlier. "Is that your family?"

He raised his eyebrows. "Yes. But I'm surprised you recognized them."

She shrugged. "I was just going off the fact that the man and baby were blue. What species is your mom?"

"She's a Vatosangan, from a planet two solar systems away from Kirenai Prime."

"Do Kirenai always buy their females? Like you tried to buy me?"

He laughed. "No, my parents met at a game of *bacca*. She accidentally hit him with a disk. He, of course, fell immediately in love."

Georgie took another drink. So aliens could fall in love. *Just not with me.* She pointed to an ornately carved pink box on another shelf. "What are all those other things?"

Arazhi rose and picked up the box. "Things I've collected during my travels. This is a *G'naxian tolonovone*. An antique."

He traced a raised curve on the lid and the box seemed to open like the petals of a rose. Pulling one petal free, he ran the slightly pointed tip down the outside of her arm, leaving a trail of golden light on her skin.

Shock rippled through her. She ran her fingers over the light, expecting it to wipe away, but it seemed to be embedded beneath her skin like a tattoo. She had a black tattoo of rosebuds in a wreath of leaves around her ankle that was supposed to be in color, but the needle had hurt too much, and she'd never gone back to finish it. "That's amazing. How long does it last?"

Arazhi selected a second petal and tapped it alongside the line, creating glowing pink dots this time. "With this device, the patterns only last a day or so. New technology can make them more or less permanent, though you must be careful with your patterns."

"Why?"

A dimple appeared on Arazhi's cheek as he removed a third petal and made small orange swishes around each of the pink dots. "G'naxians use light to communicate attraction and arousal."

She found it suddenly hard to breathe. The way his fingers held the petal, dancing it across her skin, was mesmerizing. She wanted him to paint her whole body. "What is the pattern you're painting now?"

"I'm not familiar with their traditional patterns." He traced one finger over the swirling lines. "I simply enjoy making my own." His midnight eyes rose to meet hers. "Will you allow me to use more of you as a canvas?"

She nodded mutely, accepting his hand to help her stand. He moved behind her and slid her zipper down, loosening the straps of her dress, letting the fabric slide down her body to the floor. He unfastened her bra and dropped it, too, then rolled her panties down her hips.

Breathless, she stepped out of them, feeling his gaze assess her naked body before he began painting, dappling her shoulders, outlining her buttocks, painting her toes. He smoothed wide swathes of gold light up the sides of her belly, circled her navel, and tipped her nipples in pink. The only touch he made to her face was her lips, a brief flutter of sensation, and she didn't even know what color they might be.

He stepped back and smiled, closing the petals back into a box. "You look like a G'naxian goddess."

Georgie looked down her front, taking in the vibrant display of color. "Do you have a mirror?"

"Of course." Arazhi moved to the wall and touched it. The spaces between the ribs in the walls, floor, and ceiling suddenly changed from lavender to reflective, like hundreds of mirrors.

"Whoa." She took a step back, slightly dizzy as she was faced with a thousand versions of her glowing self. "This feels like a funhouse."

"What's a funhouse? The word implies enjoyment, but you do not sound pleased."

"It's okay, I was just startled." She stepped closer, focusing on one image of herself. It was hard to get a true picture when there were reflections upon reflections of multi-colored glowing lines. "A funhouse is something they have at carnivals. Kind of hard to explain, but the gist is to disorient people. A lot of them have a mirror room, but they also have obstacle courses, moving stairs or halls, and the spooky ones have creatures that jump out and try to frighten you."

"That does not sound fun at all." The mirrors disappeared.

"Humans enjoy a bit of adrenaline now and then. A funhouse is pretty benign compared to other things thrill seekers do." She smiled. "Can you put a mirror on just one wall?"

"Here. I'll show you how." He took her hand, pulling her to where he'd been standing, and placed her palm on the wall. "Do you feel this?"

All she could pay attention to was his warm skin against hers, but she tried to feel what he was talking about. "I'm not sure."

He guided her fingers over raised bumps of differing sizes and shapes. The sensation reminded her of braille on an elevator button. "You can see the texture difference, as well."

She circled one bump with her fingertip, and the lighting in the room brightened. "How do you tell which ones do what?"

"By size and shape, of course."

Of course, she thought wryly. She squinted at the bumps and ran her finger across an elongated oval. A slight breeze wafted through the room, smelling of wintergreen.

"That's ventilation. This is the mirror control." He pointed to a cluster of three small bumps. "To get a single mirror, touch one raised spot twice."

She did as instructed, and one wall became a mirror. Smiling, she turned and looked at herself once more. The glowing lines over her skin weren't as garish as she'd first imagined, but the outlines along her hips and breasts definitely accentuated her curves. "Do you have any photos of G'naxians? I'd like to know who I'm ruling over if I'm going to be a goddess."

He laughed. "I believe so." He went to one of his shelves. "Let me see…"

As he was looking, a voice seemed to come out of nowhere, uttering syllables she didn't understand. Then the floor shuddered as if they were having an earthquake.

"What just happened?" Georgie clutched her arms over her naked breasts, moving toward her discarded clothing.

Arazhi turned to her with a smile. "We have arrived."

$\mathcal{A}$razhi let Georgie dress and then led her to the bridge where the view screen showed the curved blue and purple horizon of Kirenai Prime. *Home*. He was anxious to find out if his father was all right, but torn because his time with Georgie felt far too short. Now it would be back to duty for him, searching for a woman to bear his child. And as the first human arriving on Kirenai Prime through official channels, Georgie would be sought after as a rare bed partner.

Jealousy rose in him as he thought about her in another Kirenai's bed.

Georgie moved close enough to brush shoulders with him and looked at the view screen. She let out an appreciative sigh. "Is that your planet?"

He loved having her at his side. Loved feeling her awe. He would like nothing more than to show her the universe, if only to experience it again through her eyes. "Yes. Welcome to Kirenai Prime."

"It's beautiful." She traced a swirl of white clouds obscuring the surface of the planet with one fingertip. "I wish I could stay and see it, but I really want to check on my friends. How soon can we turn around?"

Arazhi's heart fell. He'd hoped their time together might've made her want more. *Just put her on a ship and send her home.* But he balked at the idea of her spending the return trip with another Kirenai. If he had to go back to Earth for another female, he might as well be the one who took her. "Would you mind if I visited my father first?"

A dark wave of guilt flooded his Iki'i. "Of course," she blurted.

Her compassion moved him. She hardly knew him, and yet she cared. He wanted to ease her guilt. "The communication system can sync now. Let me see if I can contact my security officer. He's still on your planet and should be able to provide an update."

The connection took a few moments before Zhiruto's image appeared on the screen. He was still bare-chested, but his features had shifted, so he now had a slightly crooked nose and what looked like a scar above one eyebrow. "My prince. You're safe at home?"

"We've reached Kirenai Prime, yes. What's happening on Earth?"

Zhiruto scratched his head. "The transporters are still locked down, and all but one of the IDA guests are accounted for—thirteen Kirenai are dead."

Arazhi closed his eyes a moment. "That's terrible. Any survivors?"

"The Khargals and the Fogarian are fine. Three Kirenai are alive but in critical condition. A human doctor has been consulting with one of our healers in orbit and administering treatment. No prognosis yet. Any word on your father?"

"We're still in orbit. I'll contact you again after I see him."

Zhiruto nodded. "Arazhi, I believe our suspect may be a *burendo*. It's the only explanation for how he's evading detection."

Arazhi frowned. Although Kirenai could assume different forms, altering one's coloration outside of various hues of blue was a rare skill. *Burendo* could change color as well as shape, allowing them to blend in with local populations with extreme success. They were often hired as spies or assassins. "I thought the

IDA had screened the guests. How did a *burendo* get an invitation?"

"I don't know yet." Zhiruto pulled back to show a woman sitting on a sofa next to a large, furry reddish quadruped with floppy ears and a long muzzle. The creature had its head in her lap, and she was rubbing its ears. "This human is a member of local law enforcement. She has a plan to get us back onto the site to look for leads."

Georgie shouldered in closer to see the screen. "Lora?"

The woman's eyes widened, and she shot to her feet, moving next to Zhiruto. "Georgie? Where are you? What's going on with your skin?"

"Oh." Georgie looked at her glowing forearms. "It's painted on, don't worry. I'm fine. What's happening there? Is everyone okay?"

"Depends on your definition of okay. No humans are dead, but the aliens are understandably upset. It doesn't help that the NSA quarantined everyone for nearly two days. The aliens who are still alive are locked down." She shot a wary glance at Zhiruto. "Except this one. He managed to escape and asked for my help finding the murderer." She frowned, scanning the background through the camera. "Where are you, anyway?"

"I'm currently orbiting an alien planet, believe it or not." Georgie laughed, sending a shiver of discomfort across Arazhi's Iki'i. "I'm heading back to Earth now. I should arrive in a few days."

"Girl, don't." Lora held up a palm. "The NSA's been looking for you. They consider you a person of interest, and they're assholes. You do not want to end up in their hands. Plus, if more aliens show up, they'll tighten security again and mess up my plan to get back inside the park."

Arazhi allowed himself a smile. As much as he wanted to grant Georgie's wish to be reunited with her friends, he wouldn't be upset if this woman convinced her to stay with him longer.

Georgie looked at him. For a moment, he worried she knew what he was thinking. Then she turned back to the screen. "I guess I can stay here a while. But I'll be in touch. Take care of yourself, okay?"

"You, too." Lora blew her a kiss.

Zhiruto's face took over the screen again. "Glad to see you got your human off planet."

Arazhi nodded. Though he'd mistakenly assumed Georgie was to be his bondservant, he was glad he'd spirited her away from the trouble back on Earth. With an assassin on the loose, who knew what might've happened to anyone connected to the prince? Now he just needed Zhiruto to return safely, as well. "Stay safe, my friend, and keep me informed."

"I will."

The screen went dark.

There was nothing more he could do, so Arazhi turned to Georgie with a smile. "Sounds like you're going to stay a while. Perhaps I can interest you in a tour of the popotan fields after all?"

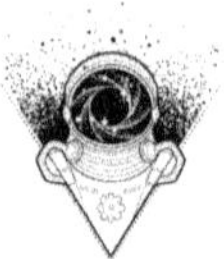

Georgie stood inside the ship's airlock, staring down the landing ramp at the alien landscape. The sun outside seemed brighter, more white than yellow, and the plants she could see tended toward blue and purple rather than green. Her chest felt tight, and she realized she was holding her breath, even though Arazhi had already opened the door and taken a few steps down the ramp.

He'd reassured her she'd be safe, but she was about to set foot on an alien planet. What if she couldn't breathe? What if gravity made it hard to walk? At least astronauts had space suits—she had nothing but a ball gown and bare feet, since she'd kicked off her shoes back on Earth.

Arazhi held out a hand and encouraged her to follow him with a small gesture.

Nerves tingling, she thought, *here goes nothing*, and took a small sip of air. When she didn't keel over, she exhaled and took a larger breath. The humid air smelled earthy and slightly metallic. Placing one foot firmly on the ramp, she stepped out under the alien sun.

Rolling hills covered in blue foliage spread as far as she could see. Mishmashed structures poked above the tree line, everything from clusters of thatched domes to sparkling glass high rises. Directly across the stone platform where the ship had touched down, a massive building set with fantastically curved spires looked as if it was being overrun by vines. It reminded her of pictures she'd seen in National Geographic of ruins in Thailand or South America, except the plants were the wrong colors. At the bottom of the landing ramp, a double column of guards formed a pathway toward the building.

"Is that the palace?" she asked.

"Yes. Welcome to my home." He wiggled his fingers. "Now come, *kikajiru*. The sun is hot. I want to get you inside."

Gulping, she took one step, then another, and grabbed his hand to let him lead her down the ramp. The ground was hot against her bare soles, but not unbearably, and she glanced over her shoulder at the ship she'd just left, getting a good look at it for the first time. It resembled a pale purple rosebud, the outside made of the same veined leaves as the inner walls.

Arazhi paused near the first guard to say something she didn't understand. The guard answered in the same language. He was blue like Arazhi, but his face looked more like the snout of a dog than a man, and fine blue hair covered what she could see of his skin. In fact, all the guards were as varied in shape and size as the nearby city. One had what looked like antennae sprouting from his forehead, and another had huge bird claws for hands.

Every one of them was staring at her.

She edged closer to Arazhi. "What kind of aliens are these?"

He flicked a glance at the nearest one, then back to her. "They are Kirenai."

He'd said it as if it explained everything. She looked at the one with bird claws. "I don't understand."

"We're shapeshifters, remember? These are their chosen forms."

Her stomach dropped, making her stumble. "Shapeshifters?"

Arazhi caught her by the elbow. "Did the IDA not tell you?"

She tried to recall any mention of shapeshifting in the numerous pages of the contract she'd signed. "I don't remember reading anything about shapeshifters…" Her attention slid involuntarily down his chest as the implications sank in. *Arazhi is a shapeshifter.* What did he really look like? "So… this isn't your real body?"

Eyes glittering, he laughed and put an arm around her, pulling her along with him toward the palace. "It's entirely my own body. One I hope pleases you."

Well, that certainly explained why he looked so hot. If she could choose what to look like, she'd want a supermodel body, too. "What do you look like for real?"

"We don't show our resting state to strangers." He kept walking without glancing at her.

A wash of disappointment filled her as she recalled the intimate ways he'd touched her, not once, but many times. He'd even painted her in tattoos that still glowed upon her skin. "Oh. I thought we were more than strangers."

He sighed and leaned closer, his arm still around her. "I prefer not to talk in front of the guards."

His words eased her concern enough to keep her moving.

He dropped his arm from her shoulders, nodding at the guards as they passed. Entering a large gate in the stone wall, they moved through a courtyard shaded by a thick canopy of blue leaves. A tiny brook trickled between scaled gray tree trunks, and clusters of white and yellow flowers grew here and there. The path they were on looked like white pea gravel with a pearly sheen, and she bent to pick one up. She could swear to God it was an actual pearl. "Is this real?"

Arazhi had continued on without her, apparently anxious to check on his father. "Is what real?"

"Never mind." She clasped the pearl in her fist and hurried after him. She would ask him about it later.

He pushed open a door that looked similar to the same leaf-like material of the ship. A diminutive person of indistinct gender met them, bowing low and jabbering something.

Arazhi nodded and nudged Georgie forward. "Deshel will show you to my room. I'll be along soon."

Then he strode away without a backward glance.

Georgie gaped after him. She'd thought she'd be meeting his father. Instead, she felt like she'd been kicked to the curb. *Of course he doesn't want me with him.* His father was dying, not in a state to receive guests, let alone meet a stranger. Plus, the emperor of the galaxy probably didn't agree to see just anyone. Even so, she felt a little salty that Arazhi would ask her to have his baby, yet disregard inviting her to meet his parents.

A gentle hand on her elbow drew her attention down to the little alien called Deshel. The being reminded her of a house-elf without ears. Waving a slender blue hand, Deshel gestured for Georgie to follow, a string of nonsense streaming from its tiny mouth.

Georgie took one last glance at Arazhi's retreating form, then followed the alien down a stone hallway. It wasn't as if she had anywhere else to be at the moment.

Deshel blabbered the entire time they walked, leading Georgie to a large room with floor to ceiling windows and strange items scattered in clusters like furniture. There were chairs and tables, but other items were baffling. There was a plush, banana-shaped structure the size of a compact car, and three chair-sized metal buckets perched on six delicate feet.

As she took it in, she realized Deshel had gone silent. She turned to find the alien's large eyes looking at her as if waiting for something.

Does he want a tip? Georgie shook her head. "I don't understand. I'm sorry."

Deshel let out a small sigh and spoke a string of obviously frustrated words before tapping his-or-her forehead with one finger.

Is this alien saying I'm stupid? Georgie narrowed her eyes and crossed her arms. "I just got here and don't speak alien, all right?"

Shrinking back, Deshel bobbed as if in apology, then once more gestured for Georgie to follow.

They passed through a bedroom into a third room that looked like it was tiled in the same pearl stone that made up the path in the garden. Light filtered between the blue fronds shading the windows, and beyond them she could see more of the rolling hills and strange buildings in the distance. In the center of the room rested a round, sunken basin brimming with water.

Still speaking a never-ending stream of syllables, Deshel made a flourish with one hand, making it very clear she was to bathe.

Georgie glanced longingly at the huge tub. The lavatory on the ship had been adequate, but a nice hot soak sounded divine. She nodded and stepped toward the basin. The tub looked like it was fed by a natural hot spring, the surface rippling slightly where the water entered and exited on opposite sides. But unlike any hot spring Georgie had ever visited, there was no lingering scent of sulfur. In fact, the smell here reminded her of gardenias and vanilla.

She turned to thank Deshel and discovered the small alien had already gone. *Well, all right, then.* At least he'd given her privacy.

Glancing around one last time to be certain she was truly alone, she stripped out of her dress and underthings, then stepped into the tub. The water engulfed her in warmth, scented steam curling around her face like a caress. As she relaxed, she couldn't help but wonder if she was trapped in a dream. Everything she liked seemed to come her way the moment she wanted or needed it. Even Arazhi's lovemaking had been the epitome of perfect.

She bit her lip, remembering Arazhi's revelation about being a shapeshifter. How had she missed that in the IDA paperwork? And why hadn't Arazhi mentioned it? It seemed like it should've come up in conversation at some point. Was he hideous behind that gorgeous façade?

She shook her head. It didn't matter. She wasn't some princess destined to kiss a frog and turn him into a prince to get her happily-ever-after. Arazhi was already a prince, and he hadn't offered to marry her, even if she could somehow offer him a baby.

The thought made her throat tighten, and she ducked beneath the water, wetting her hair. She could find no shampoo or soap, but the water smelled great on its own, so she rose, looking for a towel to dry herself.

Dripping water, she moved to one wall, thinking perhaps there were buttons on it like on the ship—a compartment where they kept towels or something. As she moved over a spot on the floor, a strong breeze hit her, seeming to come from all directions at once.

She stopped and laughed, turning in a slow circle to let the air dry her off. "Like a car wash for people," she said aloud, finger-combing her hair and enjoying the subtle flowery scent surrounding her.

Though she wasn't thrilled to put her dress back on, it was all she had, so she returned to the edge of the tub where she'd dropped it. The floor was bare, her dress nowhere in sight. Had it blown away? She searched the corners of the room but found neither dress nor undergarments. Had that little alien come back and stolen her things?

Frustrated, she peeked around the corner into the bedroom. Something that might be clothing lay neatly on the foot of the bed. "Oh, thank God."

As she stepped into the room, a scaled pink man with large slitted eyes rose from a chair tucked in one corner. His chest was bare, and he wore black straps that resembled suspenders holding up a black ankle-length skirt.

Georgie let out a squeak and stumbled back, arms crisscrossed over her front to hide her private parts. "Who the hell are you and what are you doing here?"

He held up two long-fingered hands. "Don't be afraid." His voice was raspy. "My name's Qantina. I've been instructed to provide you with a universal translator."

Georgie looked from the alien to the clothing on the bed. "Do you mind turning around so I can get dressed first?"

Qantina tilted his head, large eyes blinking, then spun to face the other direction. A line of bony ridges ran down his spine, and a stubby scaled tail protruded from his backside through a hole in the skirt.

Georgie edged toward the bed and snatched up the cloth. It was a sheet of soft, thin fabric, the same shade of blue as her dress. Not clothes, but it would do. She wrapped it around herself like a towel. It was a little short on the lower end, but it covered all the important parts. "All right."

The pink alien turned around, no expression on his lipless mouth. "Excellent. I'm not yet familiar with your species. If you would allow me, I would like to perform a scan so I may ascertain where the translator should be installed."

"How come I can understand you, but not that other alien who escorted me here?"

"The device works with the recipient's speech centers to facilitate both speaking and understanding, utilizing thousands of language databases. Once one is installed, it will not matter if those around you have an implant. Deshel is new here, however, and bondservants do not always have the latest technology when they arrive. I will see to it at once."

Bondservants. Wasn't that what Arazhi had called her when he thought he'd purchased her? "I'm not a bondservant," she said. "Arazhi is taking me back to Earth as soon as he's visited his father."

"Yes, he told Deshel this."

That was reassuring. "Okay."

Picking up a device that looked a bit like a TSA wand, Qantina stepped forward. "Remain still, please."

Starting at the top of her head, he pressed the wand against her and began making widening circles around her skull. After a few moments, he pulled out something that looked like a gun and pressed it behind her ear. A stinging sensation made her flinch. "There. All finished."

"That's it?" She touched the spot behind her ear gingerly. "I'll be able to understand everyone now?"

"Once the program has uploaded, yes."

If aliens could give her the ability to understand any language, was it possible they could restore her fertility as Arazhi had said? Swallowing her fear, she asked, "Are you a healer? A—" she stumbled over remembering the word Arazhi had used. "A Qalqan?"

"That is correct." Qantina placed the device back in his bag.

"What sorts of things can you heal?"

"We are skilled at determining the causes of many ailments. Why do you ask?"

Georgie smoothed the silky fabric over her hips. So Arazhi hadn't told the Qalqan of her problem conceiving. Part of her was grateful he'd respected her wish not to be disappointed again. Another part regretted being so insistent. These were aliens, after all, with superior technology. What if they really could fix her?

I could bear Arazhi's child. But it wouldn't be hers. He'd said he didn't intend to separate mother from child, but he'd made it very clear the child would be his. Which meant that if she had his baby, she'd basically be agreeing to become his bondservant.

She forced herself to smile and shook her head. "Never mind. Thank you for the translator."

*A*razhi hurried through the palace corridors to the throne room. The guard he'd spoken to on the tarmac hadn't had any news of his father; obviously the royal council was keeping his condition secret. *It could be good news as easily as bad*, thought Arazhi as he burst into the royal living quarters. He wouldn't put it past his father to hide a miraculous recovery just to keep their rivals off balance.

The royal sleeping chamber was empty when he arrived, but the air still smelled of regeneration fluid. His gaze settled on his father's resting pod; the green liquid was calm as glass.

Arazhi's heart plummeted. He hurried to the edge of the pod, looking down at the indistinct blue form beneath the surface. "Father?"

Small ripples disturbed the surface as the blue shape at the bottom moved, but his father didn't rise to greet him.

Looking around the empty room, Arazhi called out, "Hello? Where is everyone?"

His mother entered from the balcony doorway. "Arazhi? No one told me you'd returned." She rushed forward to wrap her arms around his waist, then pulled back to look up at him. "You're so much taller than usual."

He kissed the top of her head, realizing he was still in his human form. Altering it now would be pointless, so he simply said, "This is the form my human prefers."

Her eyes lit up. "You found one, then?"

"We can talk about that in a moment." He wasn't ready to reveal that the female he'd selected didn't suit his parents' purpose. "How's father? Have the healers made any progress on an antidote?"

She nodded, but worry railed against his Iki'i. "Yes. They've halted the poison and Elthos says he will live."

He narrowed his eyes. "That's good news, right?"

"Indeed." She placed a finger to her lips. "He needs his rest. Come to the balcony so we can talk."

He followed her trail of fear outside to the far end of the stone balcony. A small table beneath the shade of the happa fronds still held a half-eaten meal, and potted yellow *kanzo* blossoms drooped in the heat nearby.

She took both his hands. "Tell me about your female. Is she carrying your child yet?"

"Why does it matter? If father will recover, there should be no rush for me to produce an heir." He bent his head so he could look directly into her eyes. "I sense a lie here."

Her brows knit, and she shook her head. "I'm not lying. Your father will live. But…" She swallowed and tears brimmed in her eyes. "Elthos says he may never again be able to shift out of his current form."

Arazhi's stomach squeezed, and the brief moment of relief he'd felt about his father's escape from death felt like ash at the back of his throat. In their resting form, Kirenai couldn't easily communicate with other species. Which meant that his damma faced a future bonded to a mate she couldn't speak with. She'd have to rely on intermediaries. "Oh, Damma."

She swiped at the tears streaming down her cheeks. "He doesn't know yet, and I fear he may give up the will to live when he finds out. But he was clear about one thing the last time we spoke—he's counting on you to produce an heir and carry on our dynasty."

Arazhi looked away, staring at an insect with its face buried in the *kanzo* blooms. "The human I selected believes she is infertile."

Damma remained silent for a heartbeat, then sighed. "You were supposed to find a mother for your child, not another bedmate."

"By the time I found out, we were already on our way here." Not that he'd been interested in any of the other humans he'd seen while on Earth. "You're the one who told me to keep my heart open."

Damma's eyebrows shot up. "So she's your mate?"

Her direct question put him on edge. He didn't want to admit it, but the deepest part of him knew. *I'm meant to be with Georgie.* "All I know is that there's something between us. I want to make her happy."

Sighing, Damma looked him over, as if assessing his current form for flaws. "Well, I suppose that explains why you showed up in human form." She tapped her chin thoughtfully. "Earth's technology is primitive. Just because she believes she's infertile doesn't mean the problem can't be corrected. Did you take her to the royal healers?"

"Not yet," Arazhi said, remembering Georgie's conflicting emotions. "She said she tried to have a child for a long time and is afraid of being disappointed again. I need time to convince her."

"Arazhi, you know what's at stake. You're not bonded yet, so if she's not viable, you must leave her. Return to Earth and find another who is willing to produce your child."

The thought of taking another human to his bed stuck in his throat, no matter the stakes. At least he had a valid excuse for delaying. "I can't go back to Earth. Someone tried to kill me at the party."

"What?" Damma's alarm sliced through his Iki'i like a blade.

Arazhi described what had happened and how he'd been forced to leave his security officer behind. He glanced toward the door to the royal chambers. "Whoever poisoned the food is probably the same person who tried to kill father. Zhiruto has the transport web locked down until he finds the traitor."

"That's horrible." Damma sat heavily in her chair, her grief weighing against his Iki'i. Then a thoughtful look settled over her features. "You know, Earth isn't the only place to meet human females. Some women we rescued from the slave ship are still with us. It's how we know about their frequent estrus cycles—"

"Mother!" His shock at her pending suggestion overwhelmed anything his Iki'i might be receiving from her. "You can't be serious?"

"I'm not saying we should force anyone. But you are a prince and quite charming. I'll bet you could convince one to become the mother of the future emperor of the galaxy."

"No." He rose abruptly from his seat. "They've been through enough. I won't treat them like breeding stock."

She looked up, her voice rough. "I don't suggest it lightly. But these are desperate times. If Aguno takes the throne, the Senburu will control the galaxy, and if that happens, rest assured that more than a handful of primitive Earth women will be forced into slavery—including this woman you're so intent on having as your mate." The intensity of her emotions was like a gale force wind. "You have no time to waste on an infertile female. Keep her as a concubine if you wish, but you must take another who can bear a child. You have more to consider than yourself, Arazhi. Your duty must come first. The fate of the galaxy is in your hands."

Arazhi's teeth ached from grinding them. He knew his duty. But he also understood Georgie well enough to know she'd refuse to become a mere concubine. With her, it was all or nothing. He felt the same way. "Georgie would never accept that role."

Yet a sickening feeling was growing inside him, one he knew he couldn't fight. His mother spoke the truth. He mustn't allow his heart to cause the downfall of the galaxy. But he was unable to picture a future without Georgie. "Give me a few days. I'll try to convince her to see a healer. And if I can't, I'll consider a surrogate."

Damma pursed her lips. "I suppose we can keep your father's condition a secret a while longer. But you must hurry. As soon as word gets out about your father's prognosis, the Senburu will make their move."

Lowering his head in acknowledgement, Arazhi turned and strode from the royal chambers, heading to his quarters where Georgie waited. He'd spent a lot of time with women and knew how to please them. Yet he'd never had to worry about how they actually felt about him. Never had he felt as nervous as he did right now. Was he being a fool, like he had all those years ago on Sireta Prime? The disappointment of that youthful encounter still twisted in his chest.

You don't even know if she's the one. But there was a way to be certain.

Taking a detour to the courtyard, he strayed from the path to a jutting rock garden. The sun still glanced off the top of the highest rocks, and he stepped onto the first sharp ledge, letting his feet sense the hardness of the stone. He'd often played here as a boy, pretending to be a Fogarian explorer, and now he relaxed his matrix, imagining the sharp noses and facial hair common to the species. Looking at his hands, he tried to form a Fogarian's short claws and broad palms.

Although his human features had softened, he couldn't seem to grasp the shape he was seeking. Thinking he might need to start from scratch, he looked around to verify no one was watching, then let himself sink into his resting form before once more pulling himself upright as a Fogarian.

But when he looked at his hands, they had the blunt nails of a human. He touched his cheeks, finding smooth skin. And his nose was the same aquiline shape he'd worn for the past few days. Human.

Which could only mean one thing.

Georgie was his mate.

13

Georgie stood on the veranda outside the suite and gazed into the vivid alien forest beyond. Towering blue trees grew right up to the palace walls, while farther out between the tree trunks, ground-hugging underbrush ranged from mahogany to midnight blue. Through a small clearing in the trees, she could see a road snaking through the forest, alive with oddly organic-looking vehicles, and more traffic moved overhead in the azure sky. Yet despite the activity, there was no roar of jets or rumble of wheels. The air was impossibly quiet; the only sound was the occasional whirr, hum, or rustle of local wildlife.

She edged farther along the short railing, keeping to the shade as the sun sank toward the trees. The few minutes she'd been exposed to the blazing white orb's rays had made her fair skin prickle, and she'd quickly recognized how easily she'd burn under this alien star. At least a gentle breeze from the forest tempered the heat.

Inhaling the slightly metallic smelling air, she reminisced about how only a few weeks ago she'd been arguing with Maise and Lora about whether or not aliens were real. Now, here she was—in an alien palace, no less—waiting for her alien lover to return. She glanced down at the paint still glowing faintly on her arms, recalling how he'd created the patterns with almost reverent attention to every inch of her body. She wasn't the kind of girl who swooned, but damn if that hadn't made her come close.

"Georgie," Arazhi's deep voice drew her attention.

She looked up to find him standing stiffly in the doorway, features slack as if in shock. Concerned that he'd received bad news, she hurried over. "How's your dad?"

He put both arms around her and pulled her close, bending to inhale deeply at the top of her head. "Not well."

She wrapped her arms around his waist and squeezed. "I'm so sorry."

He held her like that for a long moment, then sighed and kissed her forehead before pulling away. "You're a great comfort to me."

She smiled up at him. "I'm glad I'm here for you, then."

"So am I." He sighed heavily. "But I need to talk with you."

Her stomach lurched. His tone reminded her of when Josh had given her the news he was leaving her. "Of course."

He led her inside to the large bed and sat on the edge, pulling her to sit next to him. "You know that in order to become emperor, I must produce an heir."

Yep. Pretty much the same conversation I had with Josh. Why couldn't she be worth more to Arazhi than her ability to breed? "Of course. I understand."

His fingers tilted her chin toward him. "Will you please reconsider seeing our healers? Time is of the essence, and with the situation on Earth, I'm uncertain when I can return you."

To exchange for a new female, she finished the sentence in her mind. Jealousy jabbed her heart like a white-hot poker, and she had to remind herself to focus on the good things she had on Earth. Parents who loved her, friends, a business... well, she hoped she still had a business after the debacle at the auction.

But what if his healers can actually fix me? Arazhi was gorgeous, wealthy, artistic. He even knew how to be forceful without being an ass—something most human men never learned. And the way he tended her every need told her he'd make a wonderful father.

Looking into his eyes, she saw hope there that mirrored her own. She bit her lip, resisting the urge to say yes and chance another heartbreak. Yet she also couldn't seem to say no. The silence stretched. *Yes. Say yes.* But the word remained a lump in her throat.

As if sensing her teetering, he released her chin and made a sweeping gesture toward the palace. "I promise that as the mother of the future emperor, you'll live right here in the palace and be lavished with the finest things the galaxy can offer."

It was as if a guillotine dropped, severing any urge to agree. This wasn't a romantic offer or even an offer of partnership as a co-parent. He was offering to pay her to produce his child. She yanked her hand from his and stood, looking down on the muscled blue alien. "I have no desire to become a brood mare, well-kept or not. I want a husband."

He rose slowly, eyes becoming slits. "I should've known."

Alarmed at the sight of this new side to Arazhi, she asked, "Known what?"

"You're no different than the others." His lips curled into a sneer. "Only better at distracting me from your lies with your emotions. Are you truly even barren? Or is that just a ploy?"

She frowned and shook her head. "A ploy? For what?"

He stepped forward until he loomed over her, looking down into her upturned face. "To become queen."

"To…" She gaped at him. "You think I orchestrated all of this to become a queen?" Planting her hands against his chest, she shoved. He remained solidly in place. She glared, refusing to back down. "You're the one who abducted me, remember?"

His fathomless dark eyes bored straight into her soul. "You were in charge of the auction."

"So? I didn't force you to bid on me." Her breath heaved. How dare he put her through all this, then accuse her of being deceitful? "I didn't even know you were a prince until we were already on route to your planet."

His nostrils flared, as if trying to sniff out the truth. Then his brows drew together, and he took a step back. "Do you truly have no desire for the throne?"

"I couldn't care less about some throne in a galaxy far, far away." She waved a hand at the darkening sky out the windows, noting the fading swirls of light Arazhi'd tattooed on her skin. She'd been a fool to imagine he wanted more than her body and its ability to bear children. *In*ability, she reminded herself, covering her mouth with one hand and fighting a blur of tears. Her heart felt like it was about to break into pieces. "I want a husband who loves me—regardless of whether I can bear him a child or not."

Arazhi's features softened, and he stared at her as if awestruck. "I've misjudged you."

She dropped her hand from her mouth, balling it into a fist and trying to summon more indignation. But her words only emerged as a whisper, "Damn right you've misjudged me."

Slowly sinking to one knee in front of her, he took her clenched hand. "Can you forgive me?"

She jerked her fist away, wishing she was ballsy enough to punch him in the face. "Why should I?"

"Because I love you."

Time stopped for a moment. She blinked. Mere seconds ago, he'd accused her of deceit. Then there was the fact they'd only just met. How could he love her? "You're only saying that so I'll go see the healers. The moment they confirm I'm barren, you'll kick my ass to the curb."

He tilted his head. "I don't know what this curb is you refer to, but rest assured I would never, ever kick you."

His sincere confusion almost made her smile. Almost. "It means you'll throw me away like trash. Discard and abandon."

"Never." He shook his head, his midnight eyes full of integrity. "I wish to give you everything your heart desires. I was wrong to doubt your intentions. You are my mate."

Taking her hand again, he pressed his forehead to her knuckles, then once more met her gaze. "I, Prince Arazhi, first in line of the Yazhu dynasty, offer myself for your pleasure for the rest of your days. Georgie, in the manner of the Kirenai mate-bond, will you become my queen?"

Her breath caught. Was he serious? "Are you... are you asking me to marry you?"

He nodded. "More than marry. Mate. Kirenai pair for life, *kikajiru*. What I'm asking is not trivial."

"But you need an heir. What if the healers can't fix me?"

There was a hint of worry in his tone as he said, "We have other options. We could use a surrogate to bear my child, though that's not something I want to think about now. All I know is that I can't live without you. Please say yes."

Her heart urged her to agree, but her brain cautioned her with common sense. This was happening too fast.

Maybe it was normal among aliens to fall in love so quickly, but she was human, and she'd never believed in love at first sight. "Can I have time to think about it?"

He frowned and tilted his head down. "If that's what you need."

She swallowed, guilt creeping in that she couldn't freely return his feelings. "For humans, love takes more time." Before she could stop herself, she added, "Let me see the healers first. If they can't help me, you'll have a chance to change your mind."

His gaze connected to hers like a bolt of lightning. "Nothing they say will change my desire for you."

Her skin flushed with warmth and her knees grew weak. God, she wanted him to touch her right now, to stand and pull her close. It was as if every one of her nerve endings caught on fire. But it wouldn't be right to give in to him, not until they had an answer. If he still wanted her when they confirmed her infertility, then she'd say yes. She lifted her chin in defiance. "It might not change your mind, but it could change mine."

That same almost-smile he'd worn at the auction softened his features, as if he'd just glimpsed her deepest secret. "Then we shall see the healers. But no matter what, you'll be my bride."

She nodded slowly, still unsure.

He let his attention drift slowly down her body, and she became hyperconscious of the fact she wore no underthings below the thin fabric wrapped around her like a towel. He ran a finger along the seam of cloth falling down her front, taking the bottom edge and rubbing it between his fingers so it gaped open by her thigh. "You're beautiful in this."

A draft teased her nether regions, and she gulped air that suddenly felt thick with desire. "Thank you. But I'd like some real clothes before we go anywhere. I'm worried this might fall off at an inopportune moment."

With a quick tug, he pulled the wrap free. "I see what you mean."

She scrambled to grab it before it fell to the floor. "Arazhi!"

Both his hands engulfed hers, freezing her in place so she remained completely naked before him. He looked down at her breasts. "Many species wear no clothing at all, you know."

Her skin felt electrified, and her pulse raced. His mouth was close enough to kiss. *Do it*, her heart urged. Or was that her pussy? He had her hormones in an uproar. And he obviously wanted her again, even if she couldn't get pregnant. "But you're the one wearing clothes."

"Am I?" His deep voice made her want to melt.

She glanced down between them and sucked in a breath—his pants were gone, and his dick was thick and ready. Her insides fluttered. "Oh."

His fingers still around hers, he pulled them to his heated cock. Guiding her touch, he pushed down until the head of his shaft nudged between her thighs.

Unable to resist, she tilted her hips and let him slide between her legs. Her juices were already flowing, and she shuddered at the sensation of his ridges bumping along her clit. An unintelligible moan escaped her lips.

Tugging her hands free of his, she grabbed his ass, pulling him forward until their hips met, his shaft clamped between her legs.

His length throbbed against her lower lips.

She let her head fall back. "How are you so freaking hot?"

Lightning quick, he flung her onto the bed and thrust one knee between her thighs as he climbed up her body, forcing her legs apart as he moved. Reaching her mouth, he dipped down and claimed a kiss, his tongue demanding and urgent.

She let herself sink into the pleasure of the moment as his muscular thigh ground against her heated center. One of his hands moved to her breast, massaging and tweaking the nipple to aching awareness. His tongue plundered her mouth, filling her again and again while she writhed against the pressure of his thigh.

He brought his other leg up, spreading her wide until the head of his cock probed her slit. Teasing her opening, he spread her slickness with his length, circling, throbbing, pulsing. Then, with a single, sharp thrust, he drove his long hot shaft inside her.

The motion brought her to the edge of an orgasm almost immediately. She cried out, clawing her fingernails against his ass.

With small thrusts, he continued kissing her until the aftershocks ended. Then he drew back and filled her again, beginning a pounding rhythm. Each time he pistoned forward, she gasped, the pleasure surging in growing waves as a second climax built inside her.

His hands cupped her face, and he kissed her until she was helpless under the onslaught. When her orgasm broke, it came like a storm, a flash of lightning and a roll of thunder that made every muscle in her body convulse.

She'd barely come down when Arazhi's release triggered her third climax. His hot seed spilling between her thighs was pleasure itself as he ground his hips, ejaculating deeply inside her. He shuddered and slumped on top of her, breathing hard.

They remained locked together, his weight a comforting pressure, his fingers tangled in her hair as he supported himself on his elbows. When their breaths had slowed, he nuzzled her ear and feathered kisses down her throat, keeping his arms around her like a protective cage. "I am never going to let you go."

14

The next morning, they sat on the veranda again, enjoying a small breakfast together before the sun crept over the horizon. The soft sounds of animals and insects among the trees created a song Arazhi realized he'd missed during his time away. Being here with Georgie felt more right than he could've imagined. He'd made love to her all night, struggling against his need to take the final step in their bond. She didn't yet grasp what his commitment meant, and though he was under pressure to sire an heir, he intended to give her all the time she needed to recognize him as her mate.

He placed another *kazhitu* bun on her plate. "How do humans bond with a mate?"

Georgie shrugged. "A couple usually holds a wedding and invites all their friends and family to hear their vows of eternal love." A wave of bitterness flooded his Iki'i. "But most humans don't actually bond for life."

He nodded slowly, getting the sense he was broaching a sore subject. "There are many species like that. But for a Kirenai and his mate, there is no breaking the bond once it is set."

She made a non-committal sound and took a bite of her bun, looking out at the forest.

Reaching out, he took her hand, drawing her attention back to his face. "I sense you doubt me. But we exchange more than vows when we select a mate. To form a pair bond, a Kirenai passes along a small genetic marker that grants a mate an extended life—usually enough to match his own."

Georgie's brows drew together. "Extended life? Do Kirenai live a long time?"

He leaned back in his chair. "It's not uncommon for us to live eight hundred to a thousand of your Earth years."

The bun she was holding dropped back to her plate with a soft thud. "How old are you?"

"I'm still young, not yet two hundred. We'll have a long and wonderful life together."

Incredulity rendered her silent, and he gave her a few moments to mull everything over. Few species lived as long as Kirenai, and he understood the time span could be daunting.

Finally she whispered, "I definitely need to see the healers before we do anything you'll regret."

She still worries I'll reject her. His heart ached. He'd hurt her by doubting her motives. And although he, too, worried about how he was going to produce an heir, he wasn't willing to give up the woman who'd claimed his heart. "That has no bearing on our bond. We have plenty of time to see the healers."

"Earlier, you said time was of the essence to produce an heir. I think it's only fair you know what your options are going to be." She pressed her fingers against some crumbs on the table and deposited them back on her plate. "Let's tear off the bandage and get it over with."

The universal translator still had trouble with her idioms, but he thought he understood her. "You need to put that worry behind us."

She nodded.

"If that's what you need, then we'll see the healers immediately."

She pushed away her plate. "I'm ready whenever you are."

He rose. "Afterward, I want to take you to the popotan fields for a picnic. I think you'll enjoy them."

He led her through the palace to the clinic and let Georgie explain what the doctors on Earth had told her. "Spare no effort," he instructed Elthos, his father's personal healer. "And do it quickly. You understand what's at stake."

"Of course, Prince Arazhi." The pink-scaled Qalqan nodded and asked Georgie to accompany him to the scanning chamber.

While Georgie was being scanned, Arazhi made arrangements to visit the popotan fields, hoping to give her something else to focus on while they waited for the results. Normally, he'd take his private transport, but he wanted Georgie to experience the raw charm of the rural district in the same way he had as a child. He arranged for an airlift to drop the public viewing area, and selected a handful of palace guards to go with them; normally, Arazhi travelled with only Zhiruto, but recent events had made him more cautious, and he wanted to enjoy the day with his mate without distraction. From the palace kitchens, he coordinated a picnic lunch that would be suitable for a human for when they arrived. He wanted everything to be perfect, yet still have enough spontaneity to allow Georgie to make her own choices.

By the time Georgie emerged from the healing wing looking flushed, he was satisfied their day would be perfect.

"They said they need a few days to analyze the data and come up with a treatment," she said. He'd given her a selection of clothing, and she now wore a flowing white tunic and breezy, loose-legged pants that still managed to show off her delectable curves as she walked.

"There's nothing you can do now, so let's enjoy our day together." Leading her to the airlift, he handed her a wide-brimmed hat to keep her cool under the fierce Kirenai sun. "Here, you'll want this when we're not in the shade."

They climbed on board the small airlift, and two security guards slid discretely into jump seats behind the pilot. Four more followed in another airlift behind them.

He settled into the plush seat next to her, pointing out the window as the craft lifted into the air. "Keep an eye out for places you'd like to hold a wedding."

"I haven't said yes yet, Arazhi." She frowned at him, yet warm affection bathed his Iki'i. Turning to look out the window, she added, "But planning an alien wedding could be fun."

Thinking perhaps she was homesick, he said, "We can hold our wedding on Earth, if you like. Or if you prefer, I'll have our fleet bring your friends and family here."

"They can come here?" She gave him a doubtful look. "All of them? Because my Aunt Billie has at least a dozen cousins and their families she'll want to invite."

"Invite as many as you like, *kikajiru*. You can plan the entire event."

The short flight to the mountainous region where the popotan grew was smooth, and he pointed out a few key landmarks poking up from the thick vegetation covering the planet.

They landed near the public tourist clearing with a grand view of the mountainside, and he escorted her toward a shaded area where people gathered to eat and enjoy the vista. The cool, spicy scent of *ukimi* ice drifted toward them from a nearby food cart.

She kept close to his side, clearly self-conscious under the open stares of the other visitors. "Are we going to eat here?"

"Not here. I'm going to take you to where we used to picnic when I was a child. But I wanted to give you the full experience." Family picnics were one of his fondest memories of childhood, and he hoped Georgie would be willing to continue the tradition once they had a child of their own.

He pointed toward the rows of massive, lavender leaves lining the contours of the mountain like spiny dorsal fins. "The popotan plants always face the sun. I got lost among the rows once as a child because they'd rotated. I thought it was a great game, but my parents were terrified. They sent out half the palace guard to find me."

Georgie smiled. "Sounds like me and my mom when she'd take me clothes shopping at K-Mart. I loved hiding among the clothes racks, and she'd get so mad."

Taking her elbow, he led her toward the path that zig-zagged up the mountain to the fields. Along the trail, the clear domes of *teozhisa*—traditional bubble-shaped hover carts—trundled between the foliage. Normally, he'd take a private craft to the picnic, but he wanted Georgie to have the full experience. "Would you like to walk? Or we can take a *teozhisa*." He gestured to a waiting cart, its driver nearly hidden in the small compartment below the passenger cab. The bubble-shaped cab itself allowed passengers a full view of their surroundings.

Arazhi planned to stop at an overlook off the beaten path. There was a lovely waterfall nearby, and the popotan were exceptionally vibrant in the area. Two guards had taken the airlift to get there ahead of them and set up a picnic lunch.

"I'd prefer to ride. I'm still not used to this heat." Her pink cheeks glowed with perspiration, reminding him of how she looked after intense lovemaking. His human anatomy stiffened, and he had to reign in his desire. Time enough for that once they'd reached his private picnic area.

"Of course." He signaled one of his guards to make arrangements.

Two of his men boarded the first *teozhisa*, starting out ahead. The guard bowed toward Arazhi and stepped away from the next driver, signifying the fare had been paid, and moved to the next driver in line to arrange transportation for himself and his partner.

One hand against the small of Georgie's back, Arazhi guided her forward and opened the door, revealing a padded bench seat inside.

The slim Kirenai driver peeked up from his compartment, obviously nervous about driving his prince but hiding his emotions well.

Arazhi acknowledged him with a nod, then squeezed in next to Georgie, placing his arm around her shoulders as the *teozhisa* started forward with a small lurch. The forest to either side was verdant with deep violet vines and mahogany flowers with yellow throats, and they passed quickly by several groups hiking up on foot as they followed switchback after switchback.

The passenger compartment tilted precariously each time, and Georgie clutched his arm. "Does he have to go so fast?"

"He's probably nervous about transporting royalty." Arazhi spoke into the intercom, asking the driver to slow down.

Either the intercom was broken, or the driver was too nervous to comply. They broke from the forest into the lower edge of the fields, rounding another corner onto a rocky ledge. The view down the mountainside opened up, showing an ocean of blue forest with the occasional spire or cluster of rounded huts.

"It's amazing that you can build spaceships out of these plants," Georgie said.

"It has something to do with their sensitivity to light. I can arrange for you to speak with a scientist if you're interested."

She laughed. "I probably wouldn't understand most of what he said."

The *teozhisa* rocked again, and Arazhi scowled. It had been a long time since he'd been here, but he was fairly certain they'd taken a wrong turn. The guards must not have been clear in their directions.

I miss Zhiruto. He pounded harder against the floorboard. "Where are you taking us? We don't need to leave the trail."

The driver didn't stop. In fact, he seemed to speed up.

"What's happening? Where are we going?" Georgie clung to his arm. Her fear stabbed into his Iki'i and made his already racing heart pound faster.

He opened the door a crack and leaned down to look into the driver's compartment. The compartment was empty, and the rocky ground was flying by at breakneck speed.

"*Kuzara,*" he swore, pulling himself back into the cab. "Something happened to the driver. I need to engage the brakes."

But it was too late. The ground suddenly dropped out from beneath them, and they were no longer hovering —they were falling. The *teozhisa* tilted, flinging them both forward against the windshield. Below, jagged rocks loomed like teeth.

There was no time to think. He had to protect his mate. Relaxing into his resting state, he engulfed her.

He could only hope his own body was enough to save her.

15

Georgie opened her eyes to find a scaled pink muzzle filling her view. She gasped, and the Qalqan drew back, forcing her to squint against the bright lights overhead. Last she remembered, they'd been hurtling over a cliff, then she'd felt like she'd been encased in shrink wrap, the same sensation she'd had when Arazhi'd transported her to his ship. Now she was in the palace clinic, reclining on the same small bed she'd been on earlier for her scans.

The healer who'd woken her held a strange, multi-pronged device, and in a raspy voice like nails on a chalkboard said, "She's conscious."

A second Qalqan moved into view, his black skirt and suspenders the same as the first one wore. Were these the same healers who'd done her scans earlier? She wished they wore nametags or something. She was embarrassed to admit she couldn't tell them apart.

"What happened?" Her eyes felt watery, and every muscle in her body was on fire.

"You were in an accident," the first healer said. "You've been unconscious for two days."

The other healer rasped, "I'll let the security team know you're awake. They want to speak with you."

"Two days?" The last thing she remembered was the ground rising toward them at breakneck speed. It was a miracle she was alive. *Those bubble carts must have some seriously high-tech safety measures.*

She wiggled her fingers and toes, lifting both hands to see if anything was broken. Although she ached, she appeared to be intact. Grimacing, she sat up. Two blue-skinned guards stood near the exit, and another pair stood at the opposite doorway. The rest of the room was empty.

"Where's Arazhi?" she asked.

"He's in a regen pod right now. He took an extraordinary amount of damage and will require time to recover."

The pit of her stomach churned. How was he hurt so badly if she was fine? She pushed off the bed, pain lancing her knees as her feet took her weight. "Can I see him?"

The nearest healer nodded. "Of course. This way."

She gritted her teeth and hobbled past a pair of guards to the next room where what looked like four concrete bathtubs full of green liquid lined a wall. The air smelled like strawberries, and a slight humming sound came from wall panels scrolling with unrecognizable text.

The healer pulled something that looked like a hovering surfboard over next to one of the tubs. "Here, sit. He's sedated and may be slow to respond, but he can hear you. I'll send the security team in here when they arrive."

She moved closer to the tub and peered into the glossy green liquid. It reminded her of Jello before it had set, only instead of fruit and marshmallows floating in it, a blue sludge covered the bottom. She frowned. Where was Arazhi?

"I think this is the wrong one." She glanced over her shoulder, but the healer had already gone.

Legs trembling, she leaned on the floating stool and limped to the next tub, peering into it. The green fluid in this one was completely clear. She moved to the next one. It appeared to be empty, too.

She turned to move back down the row to the tub at the other end when a short woman with alabaster skin and dark blue hair entered the room and hurried to the first tub Georgie'd been sitting by.

The woman gripped the edge and stared down into the green fluid. "Arazhi, you need to wake up."

Georgie's brows drew together. Had her eyes been playing tricks on her? Maybe she had a concussion. Or perhaps Arazhi was somehow concealed in the blue layer at the bottom. "Is Arazhi in that one?"

The woman's head jerked up, her gaze instantly shrewd. "You must be Georgie."

"Yes." The woman's posture and tone made Georgie want to take a step back. Who was this person, and why did she seem so hostile? A vague memory of the photos Arazhi'd had on his ship popped to mind—a blue-haired woman wearing a crown of interwoven diamonds. "Are you his mother?"

Gaze flicking over Georgie's body as if judging and finding her lacking, the woman said, "I am Empress Vella."

Realizing she was standing face-to-face with the empress of the entire frickin' galaxy, Georgie attempted an awkward curtsy. Then she felt silly. Did aliens even curtsy to royalty? "A pleasure to meet you, your highness. Is that the correct title?"

"I have no time for titles." Empress Vella turned back to the tub. "Leave us."

Indignation prickled along Georgie's spine. She understood a mother's concern, but Arazhi was important to her. "I was in the accident with him. I need to know he's all right, then I'll go."

Still facing away, Empress Vella's shoulders remained rigid. "He'll be fine. But he almost died because of you."

"Me?" Georgie put a hand against her chest. Where was this woman's anger coming from? "I didn't cause that crash."

"Not directly, but it was aimed at you." With a glance over her shoulder, the empress all but threw daggers from her eyes.

Georgie sucked in a breath. "Why would anyone want to kill me?"

"Because they think you're going to bear Arazhi's heir." Empress Vella turned to face her. "It would be one thing if you were, but you can't. He could've died protecting you, and you can't even give him the one thing he needs."

Nausea rolled up Georgie's throat. "We don't know that yet. He says the healers can probably fix me."

The woman's indigo lips pursed. "I just spoke to the healers. They say they can't."

The room seemed to tilt, and Georgie caught herself with one hand against the stool. *Guess there's no such thing as HIPAA when it comes to alien doctors.* "Did they say why?"

Empress Vella crossed her arms. "Only that you aren't compatible or you'd be pregnant already."

Hating the hope Arazhi had created inside her, she said, "That's not fair. Arazhi and I have only known each other a few days."

The woman crossed her arms. "Do you know where we got most of our data about humans? From females who were abducted by black market traders to become breeders. We rescued them from slavery, but all the humans on board that ship who'd been pleasured by Kirenai had already conceived. It seems that humans are uniquely receptive to Kirenai insemination." Arazhi's mother stepped closer. "Or they're not."

The woman's words snapped Georgie's tenuous hope, sending pain crashing into her like a ten-thousand-pound steel beam. She couldn't breathe. This was exactly what she'd feared when Arazhi'd suggested they try to let the healers fix her.

Ripples shuddered across the surface of the green fluid behind the empress. The surface parted, and Arazhi's face appeared. His eyes remained closed, but his lips moved. "Damma, stop."

Empress Vella didn't even look in his direction. "You can't protect her, Arazhi. She deserves to know what will happen." She moved forward again until she stood an arm's length away from Georgie. "You have more than your own future to consider. Remember the slaves I mentioned? If my son fails to produce an heir, our enemies will seize control of the galaxy, and the first thing they'll do is force every fertile female on your planet to become a breeder. A slave."

Cold shock crashed into Georgie. Then she remembered the auction, and her shock turned to anger. "Isn't that what your son already tried to do at my auction?"

This time Arazhi spoke, his face still the only part of him showing. "That was a misunderstanding. A bondservant willingly enters a contract, and I relinquished my claim to you when you clarified our terms."

"Our enemies make no such contracts," Empress Vella added. "They take what they want by force. That's why an heir is so critical. You have to let my son choose another and fulfill his destiny."

Georgie realized she was shaking her head in denial and stopped. Over the past few days, her feelings had grown for Arazhi. Grown into something she wasn't sure she was ready to admit. And his insistence that he wanted her regardless of whether or not she could bear children had almost broken down her resistance. She wanted to be his wife. To learn to love him and spend the rest of her life at his side. But if Earth's future was really at stake, it changed everything. How had she suddenly become responsible for the fate of the galaxy?

Arazhi said softly, "Damma, she is my destiny. My form has settled."

The empress's alabaster skin flushed pink, and she spun to look into the tub. "You already bonded with her?"

"All but the final step."

What was he talking about? What final step? And why could she only see his face? Although he'd told Georgie that his people were shapeshifters, she'd never had a chance to ask what his real form looked like. Now he was claiming to have settled. Did that mean she'd never get to see his true shape? She stepped closer to the tub to peer into the green liquid. But although the face at the surface was Arazhi's, the body connected to it didn't look like a body at all. It looked like a lump of blue modeling clay.

Georgie took a step back, uncertainty roiling in her gut. "What happened to your body? Did the accident cause this?"

His eyes opened for the first time, seeking her out. "This wasn't how I wanted to introduce you to my resting state."

"Resting state? You mean this is your Kirenai form?" She took another backward step. "Are you going to look like this from now on?"

"No. Once I'm recovered, I'll be as you saw me before. As you prefer." The surface of the liquid sloshed against the sides as if he was moving beneath it.

The anxiety that had been crawling up her throat subsided, but only a fraction. Seeing him as a disembodied head was disturbing. She took another step backward until she could no longer see anything but his face.

Empress Vella spoke in a low voice, less angry and more desperate. "I understand you must bond with her. But before you do, you must sire a child with another. There are other females in the palace who'd be willing surrogates."

"I'll find no pleasure in another," Arazhi growled, the liquid sloshing more violently. "Georgie, please don't go."

"You're not doing it for your pleasure," the empress insisted. "You're doing it for the fate of the galaxy."

"Empress Vella." The familiar, raspy voice made Georgie jump. At the doorway stood one of the healers, small pink tail twitching rapidly back and forth. "The emperor has urgent need of you."

The empress's eyes widened. "I'm coming." She cast a final glance at Arazhi. "You know what you must do."

Then she stormed out without another glance at Georgie.

Georgie stood frozen for several heartbeats, uncertain. Half of her wanted to flee, to leave Arazhi to make his own decisions. The other half wanted to rush to the tub to be near the man—alien—who claimed to love her.

"Will you please come closer, *kikajiru*?" Arazhi asked. "I want to see you. I worried I wouldn't be able to protect you from the fall. Are you all right?"

Slowly, she approached, the final moments of that fall now making sense. Arazhi's arms around her. The sudden sensation of being encased in something. He'd literally enveloped her with his own body, taking all of the impact to protect her. "Thank you for saving me."

"You're my mate." The blue figure under the liquid now had a semblance of arms and legs, although it certainly wasn't the body she remembered. "I need a little more time in the regen fluid, but I'll soon look the way you want me to. I promise."

She smiled, surprised she wasn't more put off by his current appearance. "Hey, I'm no princess first thing in the morning either."

"I like how you look in the morning." He grinned.

Her smile slipped. "Why didn't you tell me about the human slaves?"

"I meant to. It just hadn't come up yet. I'll take you to see them as soon as I can get out of this pod."

"Wait. They're still here? On Kirenai Prime?" She frowned. "I thought your mother said they'd been freed."

"They are free, but we set up a community here on Kirenai Prime where they can raise their children. Kirenai don't do well raised without their own kind to teach them."

She gulped and looked at his body once more. "Are the babies shapeshifters from birth?"

"They're born looking like their mother's species, but the males will fall in and out of a resting state soon after birth. It takes them time to develop the ability to shift to other forms."

She'd be terrified if her baby suddenly melted to blue slime in her arms. "That must've been quite a shock to those women."

"Yes. But humans appear to be wonderfully resilient." He grew more somber. "I'm sorry the healers didn't have the answer we wanted."

She nodded and looked at the floor, trying to sort through her emotions. "Me too. But at least we can use a surrogate."

"*Kikajiru*, are you certain you're okay with that?" His voice had taken on a rough edge.

She shrugged, still not looking at him. She didn't want him to see her disappointment. "It's not like you're going to sleep with her or anything. I can love your baby as my own."

He remained silent.

She dragged her gaze back to his face. His pained expression made her sink backward onto the stool. "What are you not telling me?"

His eyes squeezed closed. "Artificial insemination isn't possible for Kirenai. The woman who bears my child will have a bond with me, though not as strong as a mate bond."

She looked at the wall of scrolling text, numbness creeping through her. The woman who carried his child wouldn't be a mere surrogate. It sounded like she'd be a second mate. But how else was he going to have an heir? He had to protect Earth and who knew how many other planets across the galaxy from being enslaved. *I don't want to share him.* She deserved better. And to be fair, the mother of his child deserved better, too.

Standing, Georgie took one last look into the tub. Even though Arazhi's body wasn't currently human, he was still the perfect man. Committed. Understanding. Supportive. He was going to make a wonderful husband and father. For someone else.

Tears filmed her eyes. God, she wanted to kiss him one last time. To feel his arms around her, sense his heartbeat next to hers. But the only way he'd do what had to be done was if she was gone. "I can't stand the thought of sharing you," she blurted.

"Georgie, I—"

"You have to mate with another and become emperor." She took a step back, each word feeling like it was choking her. "Give the mother of your child your heart if you can... It's the right thing to do. I'm leaving, for everyone's sake. Goodbye, Arazhi."

Before he could say anything else, she turned and rushed from the room.

Arazhi tried desperately to pull himself into his human form, to get out of the pod and follow Georgie. But the connective tissues in his matrix had been damaged in the fall, and holding a specific shape was nearly impossible. Even the small task of maintaining his facial features while speaking had been excruciating. The sedatives infusing his regen fluid were threatening to force him into sleep once more.

Curse Damma for interfering. Georgie's pain lingered in the room, infusing his Iki'i as strongly as the sedatives flowing through the regen fluid. But he also felt the unyielding titanium of her resolve. She was going to do as his damma had insisted.

Reject him.

"Healer!" he called, hoping his voice was strong enough to carry to the next room. He needed to catch up to Georgie and make her stay, but he couldn't even configure limbs while affected by sedatives. He could endure the pain without them if that's what he had to do.

He dipped beneath the surface, green liquid blurring his vision. He couldn't remember ever feeling this weak or frustrated. Kirenai were strong—nearly indestructible. Damma was right in assuming the accident hadn't been intended to harm him—it had been aimed at Georgie. But that meant the Senburu had spies in the palace. How else would they have known she was here and what she meant to him?

Kuzara, what if they tried again? And here he was trapped in a regen pod. He had to find the strength to get out. Struggling to pull himself together, he surfaced once more.

A pink-scaled Qalqan stood looking down at him. "Go back to sleep, my prince."

Arazhi was having difficulty keeping his eyes open, let alone his face above the surface, but he recognized the healer as Elthos, his father's personal healer. "Turn off the sedation. I need to get out."

"No." Elthos's flat denial was jarring, but his lipless mouth and slitted eyes remained as unreadable as ever.

Arazhi fought to put authority into his voice but ended up slurring, "As your prince, I command you." The healer had to obey a direct order. "I need to reach my mate immediately."

"I fear I cannot allow that to happen." The scaly pink muzzle lowered to within inches of Arazhi's face. "I always rather liked you, so I'll try to make your passing painless. But the galaxy must come first."

Adrenaline shot through Arazhi. The healer's words made no sense. *Elthos wants me dead?* Not possible. He must've misunderstood. The Qalqan was part of the emperor's inner circle. *He probably just means he can't let me bond with Georgie.* It would make sense for the healer to be aligned with his parents in that regard.

Using every bit of energy he had, Arazhi pulled his form together, trying to ignore the stabbing pain in his matrix. "Elthos, stop. Listen to me."

Elthos reached a pink-scaled hand into the regen fluid and pushed Arazhi under.

A wave of something fungal and bitter flooded Arazhi's cellular matrix. He could feel himself reacting, denaturing. *Poison?* Just like his father. It was all beginning to make sense.

He struggled under Elthos's hand, tried to reform his face at the other end of the tank so he could cry out, but the sedatives had been increased. He was helpless. Dying.

Elthos really intended to kill him. The royal healer had been with the Senburu this entire time.

As Arazhi's respiration slowed and his mind faded, the last thing he thought before blackness took him was that at least when he was dead, Georgie would no longer be a target.

Georgie hurried from the clinic, grateful the hallway was empty as tears blurred her eyes. She'd finally found a man willing to love her no matter what—even if it cost him a throne—and she was being forced to reject him. Leaving him made her feel worse than she'd ever felt before. Her legs felt like they'd been strapped with twenty-pound weights, and she wasn't sure how much of that was because of the accident and how much of it was grief.

Pull it together, Georgie. She stepped into an alcove along the hallway and sank onto a stone bench. Tall windows looked out on a dark, empty courtyard. Stars glittered between the trees, and her breath hitched again. Soon, she'd be headed back into space, back to Earth, where she belonged.

Then she remembered that Arazhi's security officer had said Earth was closed to interstellar travel during the investigation. Even Lora wanted her to stay away. How long would Georgie be stuck here? And where would she live while she waited? Perhaps in the human community Arazhi'd mentioned. *The community he'll probably visit to find a new mate.*

She scrubbed angrily at the tears on her cheeks. So much for not believing in love at first sight. How had her heart become so entangled with his? And why did he have to be the freakin' prince of the universe? She'd never be able to escape his face; an alien prince looking for love would definitely make the tabloids on every magazine rack now that the world knew aliens truly existed.

"Come, human," a deep voice behind her made her flinch.

Turning, she saw one of the palace guards standing at the entrance to the alcove. His gray armor encased what appeared to be a Qalqan body, only with blue scales instead of pink. She'd seen a lot of Kirenai in the shapes of other species, but this was the first she'd seen as a Qalqan. Then she remembered one of the healers had mentioned the security team wanted to talk to her. "Are you here about the accident?"

"Yes." Although his placid, reptilian features showed no malice, this dude was giving her a suspicious vibe.

She shook it off. He was looking for clues about who'd caused the accident, so of course he was suspicious, even of her. Standing, she attempted to calm her topsy-turvy emotions. At least when she'd finished answering their questions, they could take her to the empress so she could ask to be sent home.

She stepped forward to join him, glancing up and down the empty hall. Where was the guard's partner? Didn't they usually travel in pairs?

He wrapped his long, clawed fingers around her arm and pulled her out of the alcove.

A shot of adrenaline spiked through her. No one except Arazhi had touched her since her arrival here—even the healers' scanners had been touch-free. The empress's words came back to her: *The accident was aimed at you.*

The hair on the back of her neck rose. What if this guard was actually an assassin?

She dug in her heels, trying to pull from his grip. "I need to see the empress."

"Not now." His grip tightened, forcing her to keep walking.

She gulped, looking around the empty hall, no longer grateful for the privacy. "Where are you taking me?"

"To the harem, where you belong."

Harem? No one had mentioned a harem. Dread ran cold along her spine. Maybe he wasn't an assassin. Maybe this was something else. How far would the empress go to keep Georgie away from her son?

Georgie trotted along beside the guard, trying to catch his eye as he stared straight ahead. "You don't need to do that. I told Arazhi I won't be his mate."

The lipless reptilian face beside her seemed to smile, then right before her eyes, it pulled into a real smile as the guard's features rearranged themselves. The eyes drew closer together, the muzzle formed into a nose and chin, and two ears and hair sprouted from the guard's head. It was the first time she'd seen a Kirenai shift forms, and it felt oddly personal. *Why is he changing?*

Never breaking his stride, he turned to look at her, a human face on a Qalqan body. "Perhaps you'd prefer me to fill that belly of yours."

Disgust rolled through her at the same moment as realization—the empress hadn't sent him. And he wasn't here to kill her. This was one of the slavers the empress had warned her about. The ones who wanted to make humans into breeders. *They've infiltrated the palace.* She had to get away. To warn Arazhi. "Guess you haven't heard," she said, trying to be flippant. "But I'm infertile. Incompatible, the healers say."

The guard leaned closer, his smile reminding her of a chimpanzee's. "I've heard quite the contrary. I'm told you're special."

She didn't know what that meant, and she had no desire to find out. Glad Lora'd forced her and Maise to take those self-defense courses, she spun toward him and thrust her free palm upward into his nose.

His head snapped back. The grip on her bicep loosened.

Twisting free, she spun again, aiming a kick at his crotch.

He crumpled forward with a choked curse, apparently not accustomed to his new human anatomy.

"Help!" she screamed as she pelted back toward the clinic. Her voice echoed through the empty hallway.

The doors to either side were made of lavender popotan leaves, but not a single one opened. She didn't stop to try them. The rooms behind them might be empty, and she couldn't afford to slow down.

She kept running, terror driving her body past the lingering ache from the accident. Gasping for air, she reached the clinic's double doors and burst through.

Two healers stared at her with unreadable expressions as she stumbled and fell, crashing to her knees on the stone floor.

All four guards pulled weapons from their belts.

She pointed to the open door behind her, barely able to pant out the words. "There's a slaver after me."

The two guards nearest the exit stepped into the hall, while the two standing at the door to Arazhi's room widened their stance, weapons ready.

She couldn't seem to catch her breath. Her skin prickled and burned. And everything in the room felt too loud and bright.

A healer emerged from Arazhi's chamber—Elthos, she thought his name was. She recognized him by the tiny dark spot he had under one eye, and she remembered one of the others saying she ought to be important if the emperor's personal healer was seeing her. He'd made her feel uncomfortable during her scans, but she'd shrugged it off—she was being examined by aliens, after all. Now every hair on her body stood on end.

Something wasn't right.

She scrambled to her feet, filled with foreboding. "Is Arazhi all right?"

Elthos glanced at the guards. "Why is she still here?"

One guard waved his weapon toward the exit. "She said there's someone chasing her."

"Then shouldn't you go look?" Elthos folded his hands, as if waiting expectantly.

The guards glanced at each other, then back to Elthos. "We can't leave our post for any reason. The other two are looking now."

The suffocating feeling was making Georgie see stars now, and it somehow seemed to be coming from Arazhi's chamber. She couldn't take her eyes off the royal healer. He'd just been in there. "You didn't answer my question about Arazhi."

"That isn't your place, human," Elthos said. "You already set his recovery back once. I was forced to increase his sedatives to counteract all the excitement you caused."

If there was one thing being an event coordinator had taught her, it was to always double check the details. She pointed at the other healers. "As his mate, I want a second opinion. Go check him."

"I assure you he's fine." Elthos remained planted in the middle of the doorway.

"Forgive me, royal healer, but perhaps you missed something?" one of the guards said. "I did sense distress from the prince a few moments ago. I must insist that you allow your assistants to double check."

Elthos lifted his chin and stared down his muzzle at the guards. "The emperor will be hearing about this, and I assure you he will not be pleased."

He strode toward the exit as the other healers headed into the room, snatching up a strange medical instrument from a table along the way. He passed Georgie without a second glance.

She wanted to tell the guards to stop him, but had no basis for the request, plus it was taking everything she had to remain standing.

A crash from Arazhi's chamber made Georgie spin, and she rushed forward to find the healers scrambling with loose tubes and wires. They both knelt on floating stools, hovering above the green fluid puddling on the floor. The sickening smell of rotten strawberries permeated the air.

One shouted, "Charge now."

What sounded like a bug zapper filled the room, and light surged from Arazhi's tub.

Georgie gasped. "What's going on?"

"The recirculation unit came loose. He's destabilizing," one said without turning around.

Gripping the doorframe, she watched helplessly while they worked. Her feelings had been right—Arazhi was in danger. He was dying.

The healers argued over the next course of action, speaking too fast for Georgie to understand. All she knew was she needed to see Arazhi. To connect with him, even if only visually.

The green fluid was receding into a drain in the floor, so she stepped inside the room, careful to stay out of the healers' way. "Arazhi, I'm here," she called, hoping he could hear her. "It's me, Georgie. Please, wake up."

Like a man in a coffin, Arazhi lay with his eyes closed and his arms at his sides. He was completely naked, but fully formed, a blue human. He wouldn't look human if he was dead, would he?

"We must try the antitoxin, quickly," one of the healers said.

The second healer picked up what looked like a needle the size of a drinking straw. With barely a pause, he slammed the point straight into Arazhi's chest.

Georgie gasped, her own heart seizing as if she'd just been stabbed.

Arazhi's body arched. His chest heaved. Green foam erupted from his mouth.

"Arazhi!" she called out, panic seizing her. *Don't die.*

The healers blocked most of her view, but between their shoulders, Georgie thought she saw Arazhi's eyelids flutter. His hands rose and gripped the sides of the tub. "Stop him," he groaned.

Shit. She'd forgotten entirely about Elthos. Georgie called to the guards, "Arrest the royal healer. By order of the prince."

She didn't wait to find out if they complied. Arazhi was alive. The healers had stepped back, so she hurried forward to take his hand. "Are you okay?"

"I'll live." He smiled, although she could see how much it pained him. "But promise you won't leave me again."

Her legs felt weak with relief. "I'm right here."

But even as she said it, her heart ached. This didn't change what she had to do. It only altered her timeline. She couldn't be his mate, but she could at least stay by his side until he was well.

*a*razhi insisted on transferring back to his own rooms, refusing to relax into his resting state while the healers saw to his recovery. He didn't want to take his eyes off Georgie again, especially after she told him about the slaver in the hallway. His days of being shadowed by a single guard were a thing of the past—not to mention his most trusted security officer, Zhiruto, was still back on Earth.

Almost a week had passed since the accident, and Elthos had so far managed to elude capture. Arazhi had been overseeing the palace investigation, trying to determine how deep the Senburu's infiltration ran. He'd picked a few key personnel who were not only investigating each other, but also every palace guard, healer, bondservant, and dignitary who'd had access to the palace.

"Leave no stone unturned," were Georgie's words, and for once, her idiom made perfect sense.

He gazed at her now from where he sat propped in his bed. She was swinging back and forth in the hanging chair she favored for reading, her bare feet tucked up beside her, pale hair catching rays from the afternoon sun streaming through the window. He wanted to kneel in front of her and kiss every one of her adorable pink toes. But she'd been keeping him at a distance, hovering nearby like a satellite that never landed.

Although his matrix was growing stronger every day, taking less effort to maintain his human shape, he hadn't admitted that to anyone. He knew Georgie intended to leave as soon as he was well. He felt the clock ticking and knew the truth would have to come out soon.

Suddenly, Georgie gasped and looked up from the data pad with bright eyes. She'd been scrolling through the morning updates from his new security team. "They say your father was able to speak to them this morning."

As suspected, Elthos had also been behind his father's illness, or at least his continued decline. Under the guise of keeping the emperor's condition from going public, he'd insisted on being the only healer to treat him. All the while, he'd been continuing to administer the poison.

Arazhi patted the mattress beside him. "Come sit by me so I can read, too."

She raised an eyebrow. "It didn't work yesterday and it won't work today, Sneaky Pete. I'm not getting in your bed."

Leaning forward, he smiled, making sure his dimple showed and enjoying the surge of her attraction flooding his Iki'i. "Don't you humans have an idiom about sexual healing or something?"

She laughed. "That's not an idiom. It's an old song from the eighties."

"Whatever. I'm going to die if I don't get to touch you. Don't make me get up and come over there." Though she'd remained in his rooms, she'd been sleeping on a sofa. She refused to let him touch her, let alone come to his bed. He understood her reluctance to share him with a surrogate—he found the idea equally distasteful. All he could do at the moment was hope for a miracle that would allow them to be together.

Standing, she moved to the chair next to his bed. His momentary elation to have her near faded as she pushed it back just out of his reach before she sat. "Arazhi, I'm here until you're well, but I can't touch you. You need to sire an heir." Her voice grew thick. "And since that has to be with someone else, I prefer to make a clean break sooner rather than later."

"But now that my father's well, my parents could have another child." That was unlikely, but he was willing to hope for anything. "I don't have to be the only one in line to become emperor."

She shook her head, a sad smile ghosting her lips. "You said children are rare among Kirenai, that most couples are lucky to have just one. What's the chance of them having another?"

A raspy voice from the doorway behind Georgie answered before he could, "Possible, but not likely."

Qantina, the new head of the clinic, stood there with a scanner in one hand and a vial in the other. Deshel stood next to him, bowing deeply as apology flowed toward Arazhi's Iki'i. "Pardon us, Prince Arazhi," Deshel said. "I didn't realize you and your mate were busy. I can tell the healers to come back—"

"No, it's all right." Arazhi frowned. "Is it time for my therapy already?"

"We've been concerned about your slow recovery and have a new treatment that should help fortify your matrix more quickly." Qantina stepped forward. "But first, I couldn't help overhear that you and your mate have not yet bonded. This is relieving news."

Georgie aimed a tight smile toward Arazhi and stood. "See?"

Qantina tilted his head at her. "I believe you've been misinformed about your compatibility."

Arazhi sat up straighter. "What do you mean?"

"Our scans revealed Kirenai markers in Georgie's DNA."

Georgie's face paled. "Markers in my DNA? What does that mean?"

Arazhi didn't like where this was going; Kirenai left a marker in a female when they pair-bonded with one. "Impossible. Surely I'd have felt if she was already mated."

"She isn't bonded." The healer set the vials down on the bedside table. "Her father is Kirenai."

Shocked silence filled the room.

Then Georgie took a step back, shaking her head. "What? No! My dad is… Dad. He's as human as I am."

Qantina bowed slightly. "With all respect, the DNA doesn't lie."

Georgie's face went ghostly pale, and he didn't even need his Iki'i to sense her dismay. "You mean it's true? This whole time…"

Concerned she might faint, Arazhi threw back the covers and shot to her side. "What's true?"

She grabbed his arm, seemingly glad for the support. "Mom said she was abducted by aliens right after Dad was deployed the first time. Everyone thought it was just her throwing a fit so he'd come home." She met his gaze. "It happened about nine months before I was born."

Earth was supposed to have been closed, so Arazhi'd never considered that she might have Kirenai bloodlines. *Slavers must've impregnated her mother and then returned her to Earth once they realized she was carrying a girl.* The knowledge made him twitch with anger. But it also finished the puzzle about why Georgie had trouble conceiving; she needed to pair-bond first—with a Kirenai male.

Shock made the air feel fuzzy as Georgie collapsed into a chair. Her voice shook as she asked, "But if I'm half Kirenai, why am I not blue?"

Qantina answered, "Kirenai traits are almost entirely contained on what you humans call the Y-chromosome. Only the Kirenai empathic power is sometimes present in female progeny."

Arazhi nodded. His persistent sensation that Georgie had understood his emotions made sense if she had a trace of the Iki'i. "This is good news, *kikajiru*." He knelt to take her hand. "It not only means we can have children, but that we're more compatible than either of us ever imagined."

Georgie's eyes widened. "How?"

"Kirenai females need a pair-bond to conceive, but if they find a suitable mate, they often have more than one child."

His Iki'i felt a moment of vertigo, then she turned her attention toward Qantina. "So, let me get this clear. I've been unable to have a baby because my Kirenai DNA requires me to be bonded to a Kirenai mate first?"

"Correct," Qantina said.

"If Arazhi and I bond, I'll be able to get pregnant?"

"Considering the human half of your DNA, I theorize you will conceive almost immediately."

Georgie sucked in a breath and gripped Arazhi's hand.

Qantina added, "Once the prince has adequately recovered, of course."

Arazhi could swear he felt mischievous amusement coming from the Qalqan, as if the healer had suspected his improvement all along. Standing, he pointed toward the door. "Thank you for your visit. Now please leave us."

The healers bowed as they departed.

Georgie frowned, looking up at him from her seat. "You shouldn't be out of bed."

Pulling her to her feet, he guided her backward to the mattress. "Neither should you, *kikajiru.*"

She sat on the bed and yielded to his hand pressing her back onto the pillows. "You've been faking illness to keep me here, haven't you?"

Her words held only mild reprimand; most of his Iki'i was saturated with the euphoria of love. "I was debilitated by lovesickness." Lying down beside her, he stroked her cheek, looking deeply into her eyes. "Only you can cure me."

She smiled and leaned in to kiss him, the softness of her lips quickly igniting his passion. He slid his fingers into her hair, reveling in the heat of her body against the length of his.

When he finally paused for breath, she asked, "Are you well enough for this?"

"I don't want to wait another moment to make you mine. But there is one problem."

Concern flickered through her. "What?"

"You have not yet agreed to marry me."

She laughed, pure joy rolling from her like sunbeams after a long winter. "Of course I will, Arazhi. I want us to be together forever."

He smiled back. "Then let's make it so."

Inhaling her sweet musk, he kissed her again, moving along her jaw and down her throat as he parted the front of her tunic.

Her hands clawed at the nightshirt he wore—he'd discovered wearing human clothing was far easier than simulating it—and pulled it up over his head. Within moments, they were both naked. His cock throbbed with the need to fill her, but he didn't want to rush this moment. He wanted their bonding to be a memory they treasured. He pushed back onto his knees to look down at her naked body. "You are so luscious."

She spread her knees and beckoned him toward her with both hands. "I want you."

"In due time, *kikajiru*." He bent and sucked in a nipple.

Her back arched to meet him, the bud hardening under his tongue. He loved how responsive she was, the little mewling noises of pleasure that escaped her throat. Her arousal was like a drug threading through his Iki'i, making his heart race and his blood grow hot.

She dug her fingers into his hair, gasping as he sucked hard before moving to her other breast. She wrapped both legs around his backside, trying to draw his hips toward hers.

He resisted, moving lower, scraping his stubble lightly down her ribs, kissing along her belly. Her skin was so smooth and soft, he wanted to taste every inch of her.

When he dipped down to the apex of her thighs, she jerked lightly against his hair. "You don't need to—"

He slid his tongue between her lower lips.

"Oh!" she gasped, hips flexing.

Her sweet musky flavor filled him, like morning dew on happa fronds, and he pulsed his tongue in and out, responding to her desire. He toyed with the small bundle of nerves at the top of her slit as she trembled, then opened like a flower to his caress, thighs spreading wide beneath the gentle pressure of his palms.

Slicking through her wetness again and again, he lapped up her juices until her hips began to buck and her thighs trembled. She was close to her climax, and he slid a finger inside, pumping in and out, his tongue never ceasing its rhythm against her clit. Her inner walls clamped around his finger, pulsing as she cried out her release. He continued driving forward and stroking her with his tongue as she rode out her orgasm. At last, her hips sagged back onto the mattress.

As she lay gulping for breath, he climbed up to cover her with his body. He nuzzled the crook of her neck, his rock-hard cock throbbing against her opening.

She wrapped her arms around him, stroking up and down his back. "I want you. All of you."

He needed no further encouragement. His cock drove inside her with one solid stroke. Her wet heat was exquisite, threatening to tip him over the edge. He pulled back, then ground against her again, the feelers just above his shaft cupping her clit as he filled her.

She moaned, and her pussy pulsed with another orgasm, squeezing him to the brink of ecstasy. He kissed her again, savoring her lips, stroking her breasts, thrusting into her until her juices coated their hips.

"I want to claim you now, *kikajiru*. Are you ready?"

Breathing hard, she opened her eyes. "The bond?"

"Yes."

She nodded, excitement filling her eyes. "Make me yours."

He'd never heard words more sweet. Primary cock buried deep in her heat, he hardened his mating shaft and prodded her back opening.

She gasped, fingers clawing into his back as he eased inside her tightness. He'd never used his mating shaft before, never felt the need with anyone except Georgie. This was the way he'd transfer the marker that would make her his forever. He paused his thrusting, trying to maintain control as the new stimulation scaled his arousal to new heights.

"Don't stop," Georgie choked out, tilting her hips up against him.

He had to grit his teeth to keep himself from coming right then and there, but he drove forward, burying both shafts inside her.

Then he began pumping, moving in and out, fucking her ass at the same time as her pussy. He gripped her wrists and pinned them above her head, looking down into her lust-filled eyes. He'd never felt so connected to another being as he did in this moment.

Georgie's eyes squeezed shut as she made a gargling sound that slowly rose to a scream. Her back arched, and the wave of her pleasure hit his Iki'i like a tsunami.

Unable to stop himself, he sank both shafts as deep as they would go. His mating shaft ejaculated along with his primary shaft, overwhelming him in bliss he'd never imagined possible. The room seemed to spin, and he balanced himself on his elbows above her, breathing hard until his heart resumed a normal pace.

Georgie's eyes fluttered open, cheeks flushed and a small sheen of perspiration glistening along her hairline. "That was… that was amazing."

He brushed a strand of hair away from her eyes, his heart full to overflowing as he grinned. "It was, my mate. I'm now yours forever."

She cupped his cheek, trailing a finger over his dimple. "Good. Because I love you, Arazhi."

He laughed. "So—ready to plan a royal wedding?"

Her responding joy was broad enough to light up the entire room. "Yes!"

Georgie had never imagined planning an alien wedding before, let alone her own royal, alien wedding. The event was exactly the opposite of the intimacy of her and Arazhi's pair-bonding, and the amphitheater she'd selected for the event was packed; at least fifty-thousand guests sat beneath an enormous dome of interwoven vines that provided partial shade from the harsh Kirenai sun. Flowers dangled from garlands overhead, catching the dappled sunlight and filling the air with a gentle, sweet fragrance. More flowers lined every aisle.

She stared nervously toward the end of the tunnel into the amphitheater where her father stood, waiting to signal the musicians to begin the processional. He looked dignified in his silk tuxedo, graying hair clipped to a tidy fringe around his balding head. She hadn't told him the truth about her DNA, since it didn't really matter. Dad was the only father she knew, and some asshole slaver who'd abducted her mother didn't deserve to connect himself to the royal family in any way. Qantina had looked into who might've sired her, but it seemed that Elthos had tampered with the Kirenai genetic database before he left, probably to hide any Senburu advocates.

Next to her in the hallway, Lora stood holding Georgie's bridal bouquet, a stunning flow of violet and magenta flowers interspersed with pearls. Lora's bridesmaid dress was a matching shade of magenta, and her auburn hair was pulled away from her face and decorated with the same flowers. "Having second thoughts?"

"Not at all. Just self-conscious about how many people are watching." Georgie smoothed a hand over the front of her gown. The healers had confirmed her pregnancy almost a month ago, but she wasn't yet showing, thankfully. She was delighted to be pregnant, but Kirenai Prime was hot even without direct sunlight, and waddling down the aisle would've been uncomfortable at best. The gown she now wore was gossamer thin, soft and nearly transparent as it molded to her torso and floated in waves down her hips and thighs. Millions of pearls had been affixed to the surface using some sort of alien technology to keep them from weighing the fabric down. She felt like a real interstellar princess.

Arazhi had been confused when she'd picked it out. "You want a dress rolled in pebbles?"

She'd almost reconsidered—the palace courtyards were literally paved in pearls—but the dress was so gorgeous... "Pearls are traditional decorations for wedding dresses on Earth."

He'd shrugged. "Whatever your heart desires. You're exquisite in whatever you choose to wear."

Now she smiled at her friend. "I'm ready."

Lora looked into her eyes as if to verify, then proceeded down the hall, past Georgie's dad, and into the amphitheater. A loud murmur rose in the crowd as she appeared, then died down when they realized it wasn't their new princess.

Georgie was still unable to wrap her head around her new title. How did a supermarket checkout girl trying to build her own business handle becoming not only a princess, but also the galactic representative for the entire human race?

Moving forward, Georgie stopped next to her dad.

He held out his elbow, ready to escort her down the aisle. "You sure about this, Bug?"

His pet name for her made her smile, the sting of tears filling her eyes. "More than anything." She took a deep breath, wishing her mom could be her to see her as the music transitioned to the wedding march. "Let's go."

Together, they stepped out under the dome, her curtain of pearls flowing around her in a cascade that caught the dappled rays of the sun. A collective sigh from the audience drowned out the music for a moment, but Georgie focused on the path ahead. Violet carpet covered the amphitheater floor toward the squat dais where Arazhi waited, wearing the traditional garb of Vatosang, Empress Vella's home world. Georgie'd been trying to build a rapport with his mother, despite how awful the empress had been; spending the next few centuries with a mother-in-law who hated her would not be pleasant.

Arazhi looked strange, but very handsome in the calf-length, burnished gold duster vest with a raised epaulet on his left shoulder. The vest flowed longer at the back than the front, revealing form-fitting black pants with gold piping down the front crease, and was cinched to his waist by a black sash with gold chevron designs. On his head sat a small crown of interwoven diamonds that sparkled when he moved, matched by bands around his wrists and a sprinkle of diamonds along his epaulet.

Next to him stood his Best Man, Zhiruto, wearing a tuxedo from Earth, his long blue hair pulled into a man-bun on top of his head. It was the first time she'd seen Arazhi's security officer fully clothed since he'd arrived on Kirenai Prime. She glanced at Lora, who also waited on the dais. As she'd suspected, Lora wasn't even looking in her direction—she was focused on Zhiruto. Georgie'd been getting a strange vibe from them whenever they were together. Most of the time, they acted as if they hated each other, but then Lora would catch her friend sneaking longing glances.

"Did he do something wrong?" Georgie had asked soon after her friend arrived. She knew Lora and Zhiruto had worked together trying to track down the assassin on Earth.

Lora had looked away, but not before Georgie caught the flash of pain in her friend's eyes. "I can't talk about it yet."

Georgie hated to think Arazhi's best friend might've done something terrible. Even more, she hated seeing her friend like this. "I can ask Arazhi to dismiss him."

"No!" Lora had shaken her head emphatically and grasped Georgie's hand. "Please, don't say anything to the prince. This is entirely on me."

"What did you do?"

"It's complicated." Lora's lips pressed tightly together, and Georgie could tell she wanted to say more, but something was holding her back. "I promise I'll tell you someday, okay?"

All Georgie could do was nod and continue coordinating her wedding plans.

Now she stepped onto the dais as Arazhi bowed low to her father and took her hand. He met her eyes with a dimpled smile that made her heart flutter no matter how many times she saw it and murmured, "You look magnificent, *kikajiru*."

Still in awe that he loved her, she let her own adoration flow toward him like a beam of light. "I'm so happy."

The minister cleared his throat and rattled quickly through his opening speech. The entire ceremony went by in a blur, and the next thing Georgie knew, Arazhi's lips were claiming hers as the ground shook beneath them with the force of the crowd's roar.

A shower of thousands of lightly glowing balloons drifted down around them like snowflakes, and Arazhi escorted her toward the exit where a convoy of carriages waited. They settled on the carriage's plush seat while Zhiruto and Lora climbed in behind them, taking the facing seat; Arazhi never went anywhere without his security officer anymore, and Lora seemed to have assumed the role of Georgie's bodyguard.

"I can't wait to be alone." Arazhi put his arm around Georgie's shoulders and pulled her close, nuzzling her temple and lightly kissing her ear. "The things I plan to do to you…"

She smiled, her heart full to bursting, and leaned into him, one hand on his muscular thigh as she glanced self-consciously toward their companions. Except Zhiruto and Lora weren't paying attention to their charges in the slightest.

Zhiruto and Lora were kissing.

GLOSSARY

Bacca - a game that resembles frisbee golf

Burendo - a Kirenai who excels at shapeshifting and is able to not only assume the form of other species, but coloration as well.

Fogarian - aliens with red hair and sideburns who live on a rocky, mountainous planet.

G'nax - a species that uses light to communicate attraction and arousal. They also have a symbiotic relationship with an eight-legged insectoid.

Hage - bald, wide-eyed alien that looks much like the iconic alien humans have circulated.

Happa trees - blue fronds resembling palms.

Hypawa - species with magma colored eyes.

Ijin'en - four legged herd animal raised for meat and well known for its stupidity.

Iki'i - empathic power.

Irn - a unit of measure. One planetary rotation around the Kirenai's sun.

Jiro - a unit of measure equivalent to approximately two Earth hours.

K'ogai - the town near the palace on Kirenai Prime.

Kazhitu - nuts that look like sticky buns when baked. High in sugar, buttery and fruity.

Khargals - gray horned aliens with stone-like skin and wings from the planet Duras ;)

Khensei - a toxin that causes Kirenai to denature into their resting state.

Kikajiru - my distracting one - a term of endearment.

Kirenai Prime - the Kirenai home planet. Purple and blue with swirling white clouds.

Kuzara - shit, damn, fuck.

Kryillian death swarm - tiny insectoid creatures that can kill a man within seconds by sucking his blood.

Matrix/cellular matrix - the term for a Kirenai's cellular mass.

Nilgawood - a tree used to make resin.

Oritsu - An expression of awe.

Popotan - the plant used to line ship interiors that provides oxygen, recycles water, is highly resistant to radiation, and can regenerate itself if damaged.

Qalqan - a species known for their healers. Good bedside manners due to their resistance to emotional fluctuation.

Resting state - a Kirenai's amorphous shape, like nakedness to humans, it is shown only to family or trusted friends.

Senburu - a galactic conglomeration of merchants who oppose the emperor's rule. Individual members are called *Senbur*.

Sireta Prime - a popular party planet.

Teozhisa - a cart to carry people.

Tolonovone - a device that creates lighted markings on the skin. Used by G'naxians as part of their mating rituals.

Ukimi ice - beloved dessert with cool, spicy flavor like sweet mint.

Vatosangans - species with alabaster skin and blue or green hair who tend to be stocky or rounded. Planet is called Vatosang.

KIRENAI FACT SHEET

Kirenai are an all-male species of shapeshifters with a natural form (resting state) like an amoeba who usually assume a bipedal shape to interact with other species. Until the discovery of humans, Kirenai required a permanent pair-bond with a female of another species to produce offspring. All Kirenai traits are dominant and located on the Y chromosome; male offspring are fully Kirenai, while female offspring are fully of the mother's species.

Birth rates have been historically low, and over the ages, the population has been dwindling. Human females proved to be exceptionally receptive to impregnation, and do not require formation of a pair-bond to conceive. This has made Earth a target for black market slave traders who deal in "breeders." The Emperor has been making attempts to protect the population.

Regardless of the shape a Kirenai is in, he will be recognized as Kirenai by his skin and hair color. The most common hue is blue, although colors can be anywhere from mint green to lavender. Rare individuals called *burendo* can effect coloration outside this range. Kirenai blood is clear or slightly milky unless infected, when it grows murky to almost solid white.

All Kirenai have empathic abilities called Iki'i which make them capable of reading emotion and desire, as well as identifying individuals within their own species regardless of shape. This is the only Kirenai trait sometimes passed on to female progeny. The ability also makes the species as a whole consummate lovers because they can take actions and form attributes their partner finds most appealing. Bonded mates assume a permanent form pleasing to their mates; rarely can they force themselves into an alternate shape after bonding.

The average Kirenai life-span is approximately eight hundred human years. When a pair-bond is formed, a Kirenai passes a small genetic marker to his mate that mitigates the aging process, giving the mate a lifespan to match his own.

*L*ora poured two glasses of champagne and offered one to the blue-skinned man sitting across from her at the table. Stars glittered overhead, and a few couples were dancing in front of the stage where a live band played. She had to give Georgie credit—the alien charity auction had so far been a success, raising more money for the animal shelter than all the previous fundraisers combined. She also had to admit that her worry about being set up on a date with a big-eyed, six-tentacled alien from Area 52 had been unfounded.

Every alien at the auction was positively scrumptious— if they even were aliens. She still had her doubts, though their blue skin looked amazingly realistic.

Extraterrestrials had supposedly landed in Beijing several decades ago, showed off for the cameras, talked to a few dignitaries, then disappeared without a trace. Most people believed the visit had been a hoax, but Georgie had insisted this Intergalactic Dating Agency thing was legit. Then again, Georgie's mom used to tell stories about being abducted. *Whatever.* Lora was willing to go along with the cosplay to make money for the shelter.

Her date wore a navy blue suit and looked like a broad-shouldered member of the Blue Man Group, bald head and all. However, his stoic silence was giving her a bit of a creepy vibe.

"So, have you been to Earth before?" she asked, trying to initiate alien small talk. She pushed one of the champagne flutes toward him, wrapping Pepper's leash tighter around her free hand. She regretted bringing the gangly coonhound along—the guy couldn't seem to take his attention off the dog.

Her date turned his gaze to her, his eyes a solid black that took some getting used to. "No."

A piercing scream erupted at a table behind her.

At almost the same moment, her date's body seemed to quiver. Not like someone with a chill or even a person with palsy. He actually *quivered*, like his body was made of Jell-O. Then he collapsed inward, reduced to a pile of glistening blue slime in the seat of his chair.

Lora gaped, then stood to pull the hem of her crimson ball gown out of the way of the gelatinous sludge rolling off the seat toward her. *Oh, hell no.* Georgie had promised there would be no slime.

Her date—or what was left of him—landed on the grass with a plop.

More screams were coming from other tables, and she glanced around, heart pounding fast and hard. Everywhere she turned, blue-skinned aliens were dissolving. A white poodle darted past, dragging its leash. A woman ran after it shouting, "They have death rays!"

Most of the alien guests had looked like blue humans, but the two gray aliens with horns and wings had perched on the stage several yards away. Now one of them flew upward—actually flew!—and batted something from the sky.

Lora gaped, all doubt about these being actual aliens dispelled.

A drone smashed to the ground several yards away. A small red light blinked from its underside and letters on one of the rotor arms spelled Mini2. *That's not a death ray.* Just some amateur trying to get footage of the soirée. And definitely not the cause of disintegrations. So who was attacking them and from where?

She turned a full circle, looking for a shooter as she dug for the cell phone she'd stashed in the bodice of her gown. She knew she shouldn't have given in to Georgie's insistence that a police uniform didn't fit the theme for participants in the dating auction. Still keeping her curious dog from burying her nose in alien goo, she called dispatch.

An automated voice said, "All circuits are busy. Please try your call again later."

"Fuck." She shoved the phone back inside her bodice and watched as women in ball gowns tripped over toppled chairs, loose pets, and each other in their need to flee.

Towering well above the crowd, a singular set of broad blue shoulders and flowing navy colored hair was moving toward the park's fountain. He appeared to be the only surviving blue alien at the party. Was he responsible for the attack, or trying to escape it?

Cursing silently at her four-inch heels, she followed him, threading between the abandoned tables. Pepper wanted to stop and sniff every toppled chair and discarded napkin, and she was forced to yank on the lead to make her obey. "Pepper, heel, or so help me—"

Overhead, a pair of helicopters came into view, spotlights panning the tables as they descended to the lawn behind the stage. Someone must've gotten the word to the authorities. But her intuition was tingling about the blue alien she'd seen fleeing.

She hurried along the path toward the fountain, following the strings of lights Georgie'd hung between poles to make the evening more romantic. Her poor friend must be beside herself over what was happening to her premier event.

Pepper spotted a loose dog and veered off the path, trying to drag Lora with her. Lora'd enrolled her in obedience school and had been training her to track scents, but the dog was willful beyond belief. "Damnit, not now." Lora gritted her teeth, keeping firm hold on the leash.

She looked back up to find the blue alien striding toward her. He towered over her despite the added height of her pumps. Suddenly realizing she had no weapon, no cuffs, not even a radio to call for help, she held up one palm. "Springfield Police department. Freeze."

He stopped a few steps away. His well-muscled chest was bare, narrow hips clothed in blue jeans, and the light stubble of a beard dusted his jaw.

Her mouth grew dry. She couldn't tell where his solid black eyes were focused, but despite the surrounding chaos, it felt like he was undressing her with his gaze. Unbidden curiosity about how that stubble might feel against the tender flesh of her thighs filled her. *Wrong moment, wrong guy, Lora.* But damn if he wasn't the sexiest man—alien or otherwise—she'd ever laid eyes on.

Curious as always, Pepper surged forward to greet the stranger.

The sudden change in trajectory made Lora stumble, ankle twisting in her heels. The leash was yanked from her grip and she tumbled forward, hands out to catch herself.

The alien averted the dog and somehow managed to catch Lora before she crashed to her knees. His big hands were warm on her bare arms, his naked blue chest right at eye level. *Damn.* He was ripped. He even smelled sexy, like warm spices with a hint of leather. Her knees suddenly felt weak from more than just the tumble she'd almost taken.

She lifted her gaze to meet his glittering dark eyes and swallowed. *Stand up, you idiot.* But her legs felt too wobbly to hold her weight.

"You are injured," he said. His voice had a smoky depth that shot straight to her core.

What was wrong with her? This guy was turning her into a slobbering idiot. At least he didn't seem to intend her any harm.

"I'll be fine. I just need to take these shoes off." Still leaning on his arm, she slid her injured foot out of the pump. But when she tried to put weight on it to remove her other shoe, pain rocketed through her ankle. She fell to one knee on the grass.

Pepper took that as in invitation to play and barreled into her, knocking her flat onto the ground. "Pepper, no! Stop."

God, could this be more embarrassing? She wrapped one arm around Pepper's neck to keep her under control and managed to push herself up to her knees, trying not to think about the grass stains she was probably getting on her expensive dress.

The alien suddenly stiffened, and she thought she was about to see another guy turn into goo. Instead, he lifted his arm, and just like in a sci-fi movie, a semi-transparent screen appeared above his wrist. Another alien's blue face floated in the air, speaking a language Lora didn't understand, then she heard a familiar voice. "Lora! Are you okay?"

"Georgie?" Lora let go of Pepper and grabbed the alien's outstretched arm, dragging herself to her feet. "Where are you?"

The big blue man frowned and pulled his arm from her grasp so the screen once more faced him. After a few more words with the other alien, the screen disappeared.

Lora reached for his arm again. "That was my friend! What have you done with her? What's going on?"

The alien tilted his head, as if taking a moment to understand. This close, she saw his eyes weren't completely black, but deep blue with no whites. His nose was slightly crooked, as if it had been broken at some point. "Your friend is safe. She's with the prince."

"Prince?" Lora gaped. "What prince? What's going on?" She took a hobbling step forward and gritted her teeth against the pain lancing through her ankle.

Without warning, the alien swept her into his arms and started carrying her back toward the stage where the helicopters could be heard winding down. "Someone tried to assassinate the prince. I must find out who."

Lora clung to his neck. She wasn't exactly a small woman, but he carried her as if she weighed nothing. "What sort of weapon turns people to slime?"

Before he could answer, a man's voice called out, "Hey! You! Come with us."

She twisted to see a pair of men in black suits approaching. Probably Feds. And here she was, being carried like a damsel in distress. *Great way to represent the precinct.* The guys were going to have a heyday when they heard about it.

She patted the alien's shoulder. "Put me down, please."

He hesitated, gaze concentrated on the men, then gently set her on her feet.

Keeping her weight on her good ankle, she reached into her bodice to retrieve her badge. "Springfield P—"

"Gun!" The shorter man drew his pistol…

Preorder Zhiruto now so you don't miss the release!

Untamed Instinct

Bewitched Shifter

Midnight Heat

Wild Child

****POST-APOCALYPTIC SCIENCE FICTION WRITTEN AS TAM LINSEY****

Botanicaust

The Reaping Room

Doomseeds

Amarantox

ABOUT THE AUTHOR

Once upon a time I thought I wanted to be a biomedical engineer, but experimenting on lab rats doesn't always lead to happy endings. Now I blend my nerdy infatuation of science with character-driven romance and guaranteed happily-ever-afters. My monsters always find their mates, with feisty heroines, tortured heroes, and all the steamy trouble they can handle. I promise my stories will never leave you hanging (although you may still crave more!)

When I'm not writing, I'll be in the garden or the kitchen, exploring Alaska with my husband, or preparing for the zombie apocalypse. I also love wine and hard apple cider, am mediocre at crochet, and have the cutest 12-pound bunny named Abigail.

Interested in more about me? Join my VIP Club and get free books, notices, and other cool stuff!

www.tamsinley.com